SQUIB

's Squib's an only child,' said Kate, trying to explain the
nely, speechless little boy she had met in the park, a boy
ln't seem to have a proper home or know how to play
games.

more different than that', said Robin. 'Just different.
ueer. How should I know?'

Y   Sammy wasn't so hesitant. 'His Auntie's a wicked
he said, 'and she ties him up in the laundry basket
es.'

one knew Sammy told fibs, but motherly, inquisitive
ith time on her hands and to spare, couldn't dismiss
om her mind. She was a girl who likes to get to the
of things, and there certainly was something very
about Squib – but how was she to find out about him
wouldn't answer her questions and all she had to go
a ring of bruises round his leg and Sammy's ghoulish
por. Was he really a rich man's little boy, kidnapped and ill-
reate ? Or a ghost? Or even, dream of dreams, her own
drowned little brother come back to them? She couldn't rest
until she found out more, even though her curiosity was leading her straight into the most terrifying situation of her life,
worse even than that dreadful accident deep in her past.

Born in London, Nina Bawden was educated at the local
grammar school and then at Oxford. She started to write at
chool and had her first novel published in 1952.

SQUIB

NINA BAWDEN

illustrated by
Shirley Hughes

Puffin Books

Puffin Books, Penguin Books Ltd, Harmondsworth, Middlesex, England
Viking Penguin Inc., 40 West 23rd Street, New York, New York 10010, U.S.A.
Penguin Books Australia Ltd, Ringwood, Victoria, Australia
Penguin Books Canada Ltd, 2801 John Street, Markham, Ontario, Canada L3R 1B4
Penguin Books (N.Z.) Ltd, 182–190 Wairau Road, Auckland 10, New Zealand

—

First published in Great Britain by Victor Gollancz 1971
First published in the United States by
J. B. Lippincott Company, Philadelphia
and New York, 1971
Published in Puffin Books 1973
Reprinted 1975, 1976, 1977, 1981, 1983, 1985, 1987

—

—

Set, printed and bound in Great Britain by
Cox & Wyman Ltd, Reading
Set in Monotype Bembo

For Robert Bawden

I

His name was Squib. At least, that was what the little ones called him. 'There's Squib,' they shouted, racing across the shaved grass of the park to where he waited by the swings and the sandpit and the seesaw, a small, pale child, pale-skinned, pale-haired. Always alone – and lonely looking, too, which is not quite the same thing.

'Squib's not a name,' the bigger ones said, and once, in the beginning, Robin had asked him, 'What's your real name?' but he hung his head and said nothing as he usually did when an older child or an adult spoke to him, so Squib he became, and remained, to all of them. To the bigger ones, Robin and Kate, as well as to Sammy and Prue.

'You can never tell which way he's going to jump,' Sammy explained. 'He just whizzes about like a firework.'

Sammy was only five and a half but he was good at describing people so that you could see something about them you hadn't noticed before. Squib was slow to join in, but once he had, he ran about wildly in short, excited darts and rushes that had nothing to do with any game the children were playing at that moment – he would run away from the ball, or towards the person who was *He*. It was almost, Robin thought, watching him one Saturday morning and remembering what Sammy had said, as if he didn't really know how to play; as if he had never had anyone to play *with* before Sammy and Prue made friends with him.

'Perhaps he's an only child,' Kate said. She was one herself and knew what it could be like.

'Too easy,' Robin said. 'I mean, he's more different than that.'

7

'What do you mean?'

'Just different. Odd. Queer. How should I know?'

'Don't be feeble! You must know what you meant!'

Kate was frowning and serious and Robin sighed a little. He had spoken without thinking; it had just been a feeling. You could have a feeling, couldn't you, without being made to spell it out? Especially when it was about something so unimportant! Squib was just a little boy his brother and sister had picked up in the park! If he was quiet and shy, there was nothing unusual in that: Sammy and Prue always chose friends they could order about. And they were both so bossy and bouncy, so cheerful and friendly, that it would be hard for another child not to seem timid beside them.

'In what way different?' Kate was sitting beside Robin on the bench under the almond tree, rocking Hugo's pram with one hand. Wind stirred the tree and a sprig of blossom fell on the sleeping baby's face but she didn't notice: she was watching Robin, waiting for his answer.

He knew he would have to give her one: Kate Pollack was a girl who liked to get to the bottom of things. Nothing else to occupy her mind, Robin thought, feeling a bit sour suddenly; no newspaper round, no shopping to do for her mother, no Sammy and Prue round her neck, morning, noon and night! Kate wheeled out a neighbour's baby week-ends but though she said it was for pocket money it was really because she liked to pretend Hugo belonged to her. Robin had heard her, showing him off to the mothers in the park. *My baby brother . . .*

He looked at Sammy and Prue who had stopped playing ball and were climbing the iron steps of the slide. Sammy leading; Squib following more slowly with Prue prodding him from behind. Squib was taller than Sammy and a bit shorter than Prue who was nearly eight, but he seemed younger than either of them because of the babyish clothes he wore. Frilled shirt and buttoned-on shorts and long, white socks – the sort of outfit, Robin thought, that looked as if he should have

8

a uniformed nurse with him or at least a rich, dressed-up mother. But he was always alone in the park, alone when they came, alone when they left . . .

'Well, that fancy gear for one thing,' Robin said. 'You'd think, tea at the Ritz with the Duchess!'

'Patched,' Kate said. 'Outgrown. But that's not *it*, is it? Not what you meant?'

As of course it wasn't. Clothes only made you look different. But whatever Robin had meant, he couldn't put a name to it now. He tried, to please Kate, but it was like trying to pick up a reflection seen in water: it splintered, trickled away between his fingers as he touched it.

He said, 'I don't know what I did mean, really.' And then, hesitantly, 'Unless it's something about the way he looks at you . . .'

Kate thought back to the first time she'd seen him. He had been standing by the pram – appearing so suddenly he might have sprung up out of the ground – staring and staring at Hugo as if he had never seen a baby before. Kate had said, 'Hallo,' and then, to coax him, 'Would you like a chocolate penny?' but he hadn't answered, just transferred his stare to her. He had looked at her for what seemed an enormous stretch of time before his thick, pale lashes came down like a curtain and hid his eyes, and it had given her an odd, shivery feeling, as if she couldn't tell, not just what he was thinking but what he was *seeing* – as if he saw something with that wide, steady gaze that no ordinary person *could* see. *Mysterious*, she thought now, *strange* . . .

'Like a changeling,' she said.

Robin grinned. 'Bit solid for that, isn't he? Where'd they find him, do you think? Under a gooseberry bush, or at the bottom of your garden?'

'Oh, very witty!' But she was blushing. She said, 'You stupid clunk!'

He went on grinning. Foxy-face, she thought; sly grin, red

9

hair, long, narrow nose. Robin was self-conscious about his nose which would fit his face one day but was too big for it now; to pay him out for making her blush she fixed her eyes on it until the grin faded and he took his spectacles off and looked away.

He said in a distant voice, 'Can't you ever take a joke?'

'No.' She felt a lump come in her throat. She hated to be teased. Bad enough at school, without Robin starting! She said, 'No one likes to be laughed at,' and stood up, bending over Hugo's pram, picking the fallen blossom off his pillow and straightening his covers. She wished he would wake so she could pick him up and cuddle him; Hugo never sneered at her!

Robin put his glasses back on and watched her. His mother said, *That girl needs her corners knocked off*. It amazed him that anyone could be so easily hurt. He said, 'I didn't mean I really thought you believed in fairies,' – feeling rather ridiculous, because surely no one could have thought that about a girl of nearly twelve, but it seemed to comfort Kate: she turned from the pram and smiled shyly. 'Of course I don't. It was just a word came into my head.'

Bit of a wafty one, Robin thought – *wafty* was what his mother called any idea that wasn't absolutely down to earth – but he didn't say this. He felt inclined to; it was always a temptation to needle Kate just because she was so touchy, but a yell from the playground distracted him. Prue and Squib had fallen off the slide and were lying in a crumpled heap beside it.

It was Squib who was underneath but Prue who was bawling. Robin picked her up and looked her over with a practised eye. He shook her a little and said, 'That's enough now, you're not hurt.'

She stopped at once. It had been all sound and fury, there wasn't a single tear. She said, 'I might have been though, mightn't I?' and glared at Robin.

Sammy said, 'T'wasn't her fault. Squib was so scared he

wouldn't let go the sides, so she came down from behind and hit him.'

Kate knelt in front of Squib. She said, 'Oh, your poor knee.'

Blood was oozing in dark, shiny beads like a row of garnets, but Squib made no sound.

Robin said, 'Not much, I don't think, but you best get the grit out.'

Kate licked her handkerchief and scrubbed gently. Squib stood silent and motionless; his pale, screwed-up face tore at Kate's heart. She tied her handkerchief round the graze and said, 'There pet, all right now. What a brave boy!'

Prue stood at her shoulder, breathing heavily. She said in an ominous voice, 'Blood on his sock. *He'll* get into trouble!'

There was only a little blood, at the top. Kate said, 'Don't be silly, Prue, it'll wash out.' She smiled at Squib, loving him for being so small and fragile. 'Mummy won't be cross, darling.'

'He hasn't *got* a Mummy. Has he, Sam?'

'His Auntie will be mad,' Sam said. 'She'll know he's been out. He's not *allowed* to go out.'

'Shut up,' Robin said. 'Both of you.'

Kate sat Squib on the ground, legs sticking out straight, like a doll's. She said, 'I'll wash your sock in the paddling pool, it'll dry quite soon in the sun.'

His little leg was so thin. So twig-like, she felt it might snap if she handled it roughly. She took off his scratched, patent shoe and rolled down his sock. There was a mark round his leg like a bracelet of bruises; as she touched it, she glanced up at him and his eyes met hers with that strange look ... She thought, *What is he seeing?* and then, *He looks so old!* Old and wise and sad, as if he knew something she was still too young to know ...

Kate sat back on her heels for a minute. Then she pulled the sock up his leg again and said, 'Perhaps I won't take it off, then. I'll just wet my hanky and clean it on you.'

'Leave him alone, can't you?' Robin said. 'All this fuss over nothing.'

Kate was surprised by his edgy tone. She said, 'It's not nothing, your sister knocked him off the slide, didn't she? If he's going to get into trouble because he's messed up his clothes, then we ought to do something about it. Take him home and *explain*!'

Squib scrambled to his feet, grabbed his loose shoe and ran off, hop-and-go-one, straight for the park railings. When he reached them he clung on with both hands, peering back over his shoulder.

Robin laughed. 'There's your answer to that one!'

Kate ignored him. She said, to Prue, 'Will he really get into trouble?'

But Prue was looking offended. 'Robin told me to shut up.'

'Oh *Prue* . . .'

'If I've got to shut up, I can't tell you, can I?'

Robin said, 'Not now, anyway.' He cleared his throat, rather loudly. 'Here come the Assyrians.'

Kate turned her head. A gang of motorcyclists had come into the park by the far gate. There were perhaps a dozen of them; big boys in leather jackets sweeping noisily across the grass in a wide, dusty arc and making for the playground.

'Assyrians?' Kate said.

'They came down like a wolf on the fold, didn't they?' Robin grinned, but his eyes were uneasy.

The boys were taking over the playground. They swarmed over the climbing frame and stood on the swings in pairs, cracking them up high. The children they had driven off ran to their mothers or stood, huddled together and watching. One boy, still on his bike, drove straight through a group of little ones, scattering them like chickens.

'Someone ought to stop them,' Kate said indignantly.

Robin pulled a face. 'Like who? It's all right, they'll get bored in a minute. It's only a bit of sport.'

He wished he was sure of that. He had once been mobbed on his way home from school. They had only jeered and flicked his tie and snatched his cap, but the memory still threatened him. He thought, *Flick-knives and bicycle chains*, and felt his stomach tighten.

Sammy hung on his arm. 'They aren't Syrians, Robin. They're Wild Ones. T'was one of them jumped at me.'

'Which one?' Robin stretched his jaw and looked stern. Then he took off his spectacles and the world became comfortably blurred; the leaping boys, dark and anonymous.

Even to Sammy who could see them clearly they all looked alike; black jackets, tight jeans. 'I don't know,' he whispered. 'I don't *like* it, Robin. Let's go home.'

'Coward,' Prue said, 'Jelly baby.' She tossed her head and her eyes flashed scorn. 'Robin's a coward, too. Boys always are.'

'Don't be mean,' Kate said. 'It's all right for you, no one expects girls to be brave.' She stood up, dusting her knees. 'All the same we can't just go. Not and leave Squib.'

He was still clinging tight to the railings, still watching them over his shoulder.

'Hugo's crying,' Robin said. 'I expect those beastly bikes woke him up.'

Kate ran for the pram. Hugo wasn't really crying, just rearing up in his straps and grumbling. Kate lifted him and plumped the pillow to support his back. His fat apple cheeks shook, touch and go for a minute whether he howled or not, but when he decided to smile instead and show his two front teeth, solid and white as new tombstones, Kate didn't notice; she was already turning away to look back at Squib. His face was a pale flower turned towards her. Too far away to make out the features but what she couldn't see her imagination supplied: the wide, scared eyes, the quivering mouth . . .

'He won't let go till we've gone,' Sammy said, beside her. 'He's not scared of the Wild Ones, he's scared of you taking him home. *You'd* be scared too, if you did. His Auntie's a wicked witch, she'd catch you and tie you up and never let you go.'

'Oh, *Sammy*,' Kate said.

His eyes were round as pennies, and solemn. 'Well she ties him up in the laundry basket sometimes,' he said.

2

THE church clock struck half past twelve as they came out of the sunlight of the little park into the green hush of the footpath that ran from the station road down to the church and the town. This was a busy suburb, only ten miles from the heart of the city, but the path was quiet and shaded as any country walk: no houses near, only the churchyard and then the ends of gardens on one side, nettles and compost heaps, and the tall, forest trees of Turner's Tower on the other. Once a gentleman's mansion, the Tower was now an Old People's Home, and though part of the garden close to the house had been kept up, the rest of the grounds had run to tangle and wilderness; the fences broken, the great trees, growing unchecked, choking laurel and holly and housing grey squirrels and pigeons and jays that robbed nearby gardens in summer, and foxes that raided the dustbins in winter. The townspeople complained about the squirrels that stripped their raspberry canes and nibbled their crocus in bud and wrote angry letters to the local paper. 'Ten acres of good building land going waste when people need houses.' But what they really objected to, Kate's mother said, what they really *hated*, was that this rampant, secret, untamed place should be allowed to exist at all in the middle of their tidy town, next to their neat gardens planted with pruned rose bushes. 'They like grass mown and trees lopped and little houses in rows,' was what she said. '*Safe as houses*, they say, and they feel that. It scares them to have the Wild Wood on their doorsteps. They hear a fox on a winter's night and it's a sort of threat, so close!'

Kate found this strange – though people frightened her sometimes, she was seldom frightened by places – but she guessed her mother was right: she knew girls at her school who were forbidden to play in the woods, and not just because they were Private Property. 'It's so quiet,' they said, 'so lonely.' And, glancing sideways at each other and giggling, 'You never know who you might *meet*.' 'No sabre-toothed tigers far as I know,' Kate said, wondering how anyone could be afraid in that lovely, quiet, green place. Or lonely, when it was so full of creatures; bright eyes in the thicket, a rustle in the undergrowth . . .

And yet Sammy and Prue, who were usually so bold, were afraid to go down the path alone. They fell silent when they reached the cold shade of the first tree and though they ran on, ahead of the pram, they held each other's hands and looked back from time to time to make sure Robin and Kate were safely following.

'You wouldn't think anything could scare them,' Kate said.

'Something has, though,' Robin said. '*Someone*, anyway. I don't know if it was really one of those yobbos down the park or if Sammy just thought of that, but whoever he was, he jumped out at Sammy and Prue. Don't know what happened exactly, you know what kids are, they'll only tell you half of a thing, but they've been scared since.'

'I've never seen anyone in the woods. Only the old gardener, near the house. *He* wouldn't scare anyone.'

'Sammy said a big boy. He said he had a knife. I don't *think* he was making it up.'

Kate raised one eyebrow. You could never tell with Sammy.

'Oh I know,' Robin said. 'But I don't think he was *this* time. He came home howling.'

'That doesn't prove it. You know what Sammy is, he believes his own tales.' Kate hesitated. 'All that about Squib and his Auntie being a witch and tying him up in a basket, he believes *that*.'

'Hansel and Gretel,' Robin said. 'That's the witch part.

Mum was reading it to them last week. The rest – well, I don't know. I mean, people are funny sometimes.'

Kate looked at him. 'That mark on his leg?'

'Umm.'

'But Sammy can't *know*, can he? I mean, Squib doesn't *talk*.'

Robin said slowly, 'I expect he does to them. Or they understand him somehow. There was a French boy we met at the seaside. He didn't speak a word of English but Sammy and Prue got on with him all right. It's something you can do when you're small.'

Kate drew a deep breath. 'Then it's awful! Tying a little boy up like a dog! It's the most frightful thing!'

'Keep your wig on! We don't even know if it's true.'

'I thought you just said it was.'

'Just thinking aloud, that's all. Thinking Squib might have told Sammy something, not saying he *did*. It might just be a Sam-story, after all.'

'Ask him,' Kate said. 'Find out.'

The colour had quite gone from her face. Robin looked at her curiously. 'All right. If you like.'

Her eyes blazed at him. 'Don't *you* want to know? Don't you *care*?'

He said, uncomfortably, 'Well, it's not our business, is it?'

'That's what people always say when they don't want to be bothered.' She wrinkled her mouth into a prune and said, in a prim, fluting voice, 'Oh *poor* little boy, what a pity he's so unhappy, but it's not *our* business, is it?'

Robin sighed. Kate rushed at things so – show her a molehill and she'd start at once, shovelling earth and building a mountain. It made him want to be slow and cautious. He said, 'Who said he was unhappy? I mean, it's not as if he was black and blue all over or covered in *blood*. You can't go tearing off to the police or something and say, look, there's this kid in the park, we don't know who he is or where he lives or anything about him at all, but he's shy and he's got odd eyes and a bit of a bruise on one leg and Sammy, who's only five and tells the most whopping *lies*, says his Auntie's a wicked witch, so please will you do something about it?'

Kate didn't answer for a minute. She made a funny face at Hugo and said, 'Grrr . . .' and when he laughed, laughed too, very loudly, as if she were pretending Robin wasn't there. At last she said, in a flat voice, 'Odd eyes?'

'Different. Not very different, just that one's more blue than brown and one's more brown than blue.' Having remembered this, Robin felt suddenly immensely relieved as if he had solved an important problem. 'It's what gives him that queer look,' he said. 'Hadn't you noticed?'

Kate shook her head. She growled at Hugo again, to gain time, and then glanced sideways at Robin. She was looking shy. 'I'm as bad as Sam, aren't I? Making things up? I suppose I just felt bad about leaving him. Alone in the park with those boys. I still feel bad about that . . .'

Robin said, 'Over-developed sense of guilt, that's your trouble! Come off it, girl! What d'you think they're likely to do? *Kidnap* him?'

3

KATE put the brake on the pram and went through the open front door of the cottage. It was the twin of Robin's, next door, but new white paint and hardly any furniture made it less poky. Transistor music floated down from the bedroom; Kate climbed the narrow stair and said, 'We're back, Sophie.'

Hugo's mother was sitting at her dressing-table which was white and gold and took up the whole of one wall. Kate watched in the mirror as she picked up what looked like a dark, furry caterpillar and stuck it to one eyelid.

'He's awake,' Kate said. 'Shall I get him out of the pram?'

Sophie looked round. Beside one thickly fringed eye, the other looked naked like a painted egg. She said, 'No thanks, Katey-ducky, I haven't finished my face yet.'

'I could give him his lunch if you like.'

'Bless you, Angel-Kate, but my dear Mama is coming and she likes to see the monster fed. I can't imagine why since it's a *horrid* sight, all spit and slop, but some people have queer tastes, don't they?' She smiled at Kate; a beautiful, warm, friendly smile that made Kate's heart turn over. Then she said, 'I've put your three bob on the hall table,' and turned back to the glass.

Kate would gladly have paid more than that to be allowed to stay, but couldn't say so. She lingered, standing on one leg and rubbing the other foot up and down against the back of her calf and said, 'I can take him out tomorrow, if you like.'

Sophie was concentrating on her second eye. She fixed the lash, blinked at herself in the mirror, and swung round on the stool. She wore black jeans, a white sweater, and looked about fourteen years old. She said, 'Tell you what, ducky, we're going to be simply dreadfully late tonight, so if you'd like to come over in the morning and *creep in*, and get him up and give him his breakfast, that would be absolutely *super*.'

She beamed at Kate as if she were giving her a marvellous present, as indeed she was. Kate said, 'Oh please, I'd so love to. Are you going to a party?'

Sophie and her husband went to a great many parties. Kate, who lived opposite, and whose bedroom faced the road, had often woken in the night and heard the car drawing up, and voices, and laughter.

'Key under the stone,' Sophie said. She smiled again, but more absently this time; Kate smiled back, said, 'Well, good-bye then,' and went slowly down the stairs.

Hugo had fallen asleep, his damp thumb dropping away from his mouth. His lashes, fluttering against his shiny red cheeks, were almost as long as his mother's false ones. He was so beauti-ful, Kate thought, they were both so beautiful, it was hard to decide which of them she loved best. She touched Hugo's soft, curly ear, sighed, and walked down the little brick path to the gate.

In the next door garden, the same shape, the same size, Robin was mending his bike. He eased the tyre on, spun the wheel and said, 'Tell Mum I've put the potatoes on.'

Kate nodded, looking vague. It embarrassed her that Mrs Tite should work for her mother, cleaning a house with only two people in it, when she had a family at home waiting for their dinner. Robin grinned, as if he knew this. 'Tell her to get a move on,' he said.

Kate crossed the road. After the cottages, her own house seemed huge, looming darkly above her. The big front garden smelt of damp laurels. Kate ran round the side of the house, past the dustbins. Robin's mother, sweeping the back step, stood aside to let Kate into the kitchen – no room for two, even in a wide doorway, if one was Mrs Tite ! She was a big woman, not fat, but solid and powerful; legs like young trees and thick, strong arms like a boxer. Kate was a little afraid of her. She said, in what Robin called her 'private school voice' – high and breathless as if she had been running hard for at least half a mile – 'Oh, Mrs Tite, Robin asked me to let you know he's just this very minute put the the the potatoes on.'

'Where's the fire?' Mrs Tite said.

Kate never knew how to answer this sort of question. 'Well, you know Sammy and Prue.'

'Ought to by now,' their mother said. 'Won't hurt them to wait for their dinner. Been down the park, have you?'

'I took Hugo.' Kate blushed with pride. 'Sophie's going to a party so she's letting me give him his breakfast tomorrow.'

'Generous of her,' Mrs Tite said, her opinion of Sophie quite plain in her face. Kate longed to defend her but didn't know how to.

She said, 'I love looking after Hugo.'

'Oh, when you don't have to, it's always the way,' Mrs Tite said, but kindly, and smiling. She glanced at the clock and took off her apron. 'Fish pie in the oven. Your mother wants sandwiches so I've put her tray ready.'

'I'll take it up now,' Kate said.

She took the tray and went out. The big, square hall struck chill after the sunny kitchen, and dark; the coloured glass on the landing window made a green twilight, like the light in a church, or a cave. Kate went slowly up the stairs and along the passage to the next flight, past closed doors. There were twelve rooms in the house but only four were lived in; the kitchen, Kate's room, her mother's attic studio and her bedroom next to it. Other rooms were furnished, the drawing-room, Kate's father's study, her brother Rupert's nursery, but no one went into them now except Mrs Tite, once a month to dust.

Kate climbed to the top floor, balanced the tray on her knee, pushed open the door and blinked in the sudden flood of light. Her mother said, 'Oh Kate, you shouldn't have bothered.'

'Mrs Tite put it ready.' Kate put the tray down, clearing a

21

space on the big table that was cluttered with drawings. Her mother turned from the easel and smiled at her. She was a fair woman, rather peaky; the sun, falling on her face, made her look pale and tired. 'You ought to stop and eat a proper lunch,' Kate said.

'No time, I'm behind hand.' She took a sandwich and bit into it, but her eyes had gone back to the easel.

Kate stood beside her and looked. A wood like Turner's Wood, dark and tangled; the tops of the trees invisible, out of the picture, but there was the feeling that they were high above the heads of the children in the foreground, dwarfing them and, in some way, scaring them. You could tell they were scared by the angle of their bodies, leaning in, drawn forward, and yet stiff, poised to run. 'What are they scared of?' Kate said.

'Can you tell they are? Oh *good*.' Her mother looked pleased. 'Why, I don't know yet. I haven't finished reading the book.'

'Oughtn't you to? I mean, if you're drawing the pictures?'

'Not until I've finished this one. You see, they don't know what they're frightened of at this point in the story. So it's best I don't know either. You get a truer feeling, that way.'

'You mean, if you knew what it was, you might draw it in?'

'Something like that.' Her mother frowned, thinking. 'Not quite, though. More that, once I knew, I could only feel frightened *for* them, not *with* them. And not even that perhaps, because whatever's there, lurking in that wood, may turn out to be something quite ordinary. It's the unknown that's frightening, you see.'

Kate looked into the picture. There were four children; three facing into the picture, one looking out, over her shoulder. 'That's Prue,' she said.

Her mother smiled. 'I wondered if you'd see that. A good face, that child. Strong, no nonsense. She'll grow up like her mother.'

'Robin says Mrs Tite was an Olympic swimmer when she was young.'

'Yes, she was. I remember seeing her photograph in the paper when I was at school. Prue will be something too, by the look of her.'

'Pushing everyone else out of the way, I expect,' Kate said. 'She's *rumbustious*. She knocked poor Squib off the slide this morning.'

'Squib?' Mrs Pollack was roughing in another figure; small, running, disappearing into the wood.

Kate watched, fascinated. It looked so easy. 'I've told you about him. In fact, you've seen him. That day you came down to the park sketching for the new book. He was with Sammy and Prue.'

'Mmm. Can't place him.'

'Funny little boy. About . . . about the same age Rupert would be now.' Kate glanced at her mother's profile and swallowed hard; mentioning her brother's name gave her butterflies in her stomach.

'Seven. Rupert would have been eight this September.' Mrs Pollack spoke in a bright, practical voice as if she were discussing a stranger. Then she turned from the easel, looked at Kate for a minute and added, more gently, 'Go and have lunch now, my darling. Will you sit for me this afternoon?'

Kate felt the fluttery feeling die down. She said, 'Long as it isn't for a book about Magic or something.' Her mother's best known illustrations had been for a book of fairy tales and Kate had been her model. She had been much younger then, a thin little girl with long hair and sad eyes. Now she was big for her age and knew she was clumsy.

'What's wrong with magic?' her mother said. 'Don't be so conventional, darling! There are more things in heaven and earth . . .'

'I'm too *old*. D'you know what they say at school? *Here comes the Sugar Plum Fairy.*'

Her mother laughed, as if this was funny, or at least not worth being upset about, and after a minute Kate smiled back, though reluctantly. She said, 'T'wouldn't matter if I wasn't so disgustingly *fat*.'

'You soon won't be. Thin as a twig before you know where you are. Now run along and eat your fish pie.'

'Potatoes!' Kate said. 'Fish and *potatoes*. That won't thin me down, exactly.'

But she went at once. Unless Kate was actually posing, it bothered her mother to have her there, watching over her shoulder. Kate understood this but sometimes it made her feel lonely. She felt lonely now, more so than usual; it was thinking about Rupert, perhaps. She stood on the first landing, outside his closed door and said, aloud, 'If he'd been eight then he'd have been able to swim. I was eight and I could.'

No answer. No one *to* answer her – or to see her open Rupert's door. She turned the handle, pushed gently, and stood just inside the room. His bed, lumpy with folded blankets; his rocking horse under the window; his cuckoo clock, silent on the wall. Kate stood on a chair to wind it, turning the hands to the right time and waiting, at each half hour, for the bird to pop out. Cuckoo, cuckoo – a breathy little sound. Kate got down from the chair and looked at her brother's picture that hung beside the clock. Their mother had painted him several times but this was one she hadn't liked very much. It was a bad likeness, she said, too solemn, too sad; he had been such a happy little boy, always laughing. But Kate liked the portrait because of the way the eyes looked at her. It was only a trick, she knew, but it made him seem alive; as if, if she spoke, he might answer. She whispered, 'Hallo,' and moved a little to the right, to make his eyes follow her. They did, and she smiled. She said, 'Hallo, Rupert,' in a louder, conversational voice, and then, looking more closely, saw something she had never noticed before . . .

She said, '*Oh*,' and ran from the room. There was another

24

portrait on the landing and one in her bedroom, over the bed. She looked at them both, climbing on to the bed for the second one, which was hung rather high. She stood, balancing for a minute, then jumped down twanging the bedsprings. She said, 'Oh,' again, but in a puzzled, slightly disappointed voice, and went back to Rupert's nursery.

No doubt *here*. None at all! The eyes in *this* picture were different! One was brown, definitely brown. The other was brown too, but if you looked carefully you could see a bluish sheen on it, like the bloom on a grape.

She said, 'Well, what d'you know!' It sounded like someone else speaking. She gave a short, self-conscious laugh, left the room, and went slowly down the stairs.

The kitchen was warm with the sun and the heat from the oven which Mrs Tite had left on rather too high; when she opened the door, she found the fish pie had burned at the edges. She took it out, dumped it on the table and sat down, humming under her breath the way she often did when she was thinking about something. Not that she was thinking now in an ordinary way; it was more as if thoughts were being fired at her from outside like a shower of tiny arrows, prickling her skin and burning into her and making her tremble. *More things in heaven and earth.* And, *About the same age Rupert would be now.*

Eating the fish pie straight out of the dish and kicking the table softly and rhythmically as she did so, she thought, *Suppose, suppose . . .*

4

'HEY, *Robin.*'

He nearly fell off his bike with the shock. He had been coasting down the path to the park, quietly minding his own business, when Kate jumped out at him from her garden gate.

'You lying in wait by any chance? You could give someone a heart attack that way!'

'I want you to look at something,' Kate said.

'Now?'

'Won't take more than a minute.'

Her eyes were shining and the corners of her mouth twitched. Robin propped his bike against the fence and came in through the gate.

'As long as that's all it is, then. I've got to fetch Sammy and Prue from the park. My sister's come for Sunday tea.' He groaned, rolling his eyes upwards. 'Husband, two squawling brats. It's bedlam in our place, I can tell you! You can hardly hear yourself *think.*'

Kate simply smiled; it sounded heaven to her, jolly babies and family tea. But Robin thought she was being superior – as if she were saying with that smug little smile that *her* house was different! As it certainly was, he thought, following her through the kitchen and up the first flight of stairs. All those empty rooms and the silence; it gave him the *creeps.*

She stood him in front of Rupert's pictures; first on the landing, then in her bedroom. He said, 'That's your brother, isn't it?'

She nodded, looking at him sidelong and shy. 'What colour are his eyes?'

It seemed a bit queer, dragging him in just to ask that. But he saw it was important to her. He looked at the picture above the bed and went back to the one on the landing. 'Muddy,' he said at last. 'In this picture, sort of brownish mud. More like bluish mud in the other. I don't mean to be rude. It's just that some people's eyes are like that, sort of no-colour, really. So they look different in different lights.'

'Come in here now.'

They went into the nursery. The cuckoo popped out of the clock as they looked up at the portrait beside it. 'This one's got one of each. Perhaps your mother couldn't make up her mind!' Robin started to laugh but it sounded too loud in the quiet so he stopped. He took off his glasses, polished them on his shirt front and put them back. He said, 'What's all this *about*?'

She was staring at him with her mouth hanging open. He said, 'You catching flies, or a bus?' and she closed it.

She said, 'Does he remind you of anyone? I mean, in this picture?'

He looked again. 'Well, he's a bit like your Mum, I suppose. I mean, the fair hair. Not like you.'

'I take after my father. But that's not what I meant.' She swallowed; he saw her throat move. Then she said in a soft, sing-song voice, 'One eye more blue than brown, one more brown than blue.' And looked at him, hard.

'Only in this picture.' He couldn't think what she wanted. He said, 'No one is symmetrical. I mean, the sides of people's faces are never exactly the same, though it doesn't often notice. And ears are usually different sizes.'

'But this is different colour eyes!'

'Same sort of thing, though.'

She said, quite angrily, 'No, it isn't. I mean, you hardly ever *see* it! Almost *never*!'

'Depends how hard you look at people. I mean, Prue's eyes are green, but one's a bit greener. Bet you've never noticed that! And that kid in the park. Squib. *His* eyes aren't the same.'

She smiled. Her whole face lit up.

He said, '*That's* who you meant he was like?'

She said quickly, 'Of course Rupert was only four, then. So his face looks more babyish. But he'd be nearly eight now. About the same age as Squib. So if you look and think of him being older and a bit thinner it could *be* him, couldn't it?'

Robin thought he understood. If Sammy were dead would he think of him sometimes and say to himself, he'd be seven now, or eight, and look for him in other boys' faces? But it was hard to imagine Sammy dead . . .

He thought, *morbid*! He said, 'You know, he hasn't turned up again. Squib, I mean. The kids looked for him yesterday afternoon, and this morning.'

She didn't seem to have heard him. She said, in a clear, light voice, 'They never found Rupert's body. My father was washed up, round the point, but they never found Rupert at all. So we can't be sure what happened to him, can we?'

Robin felt horribly uncomfortable. Dead people were dead; you didn't talk about them. But perhaps Kate didn't feel like that; she and her mother were pretty odd in some ways. It was a class thing, he thought: the posher you were, the less you cared what you said.

'I don't see what you're getting at.' He did, but didn't want to admit it. Really, she was a weird girl! All that about change-lings, and now this! 'Unless you're out of your tiny mind,' he said, and grinned with embarrassment.

She was white as chalk and breathing hard. She stood for a minute looking at him as if she would like to strike him dead. Then she tossed her head and gave a silly, artificial laugh. 'I suppose it was just the *eyes*. Such an odd *coincidence*, don't you think?' She nodded at her brother's portrait. 'I'd never noticed it before.'

That awful, snobby, put-on voice jarred Robin's teeth like a nail scraped on a blackboard. But he felt sorry for her – she must feel such a fool! He said, 'I expect it was me telling you about Squib yesterday that made you see it. So it's not odd really. Just the way minds work. Like seeing a man with a huge, great nose all covered in bumps and then seeing six others, one after the other. You sort of *tune in* to noses!'

'Speak for yourself.' The colour came back into her face and she giggled. 'I can see you might!'

'Oh, all right.' He was angry, but only briefly, because he had thought of another interesting thing to say. 'You see! My saying that just shows how funny minds are! I wasn't thinking about noses but when I want an example of something it's what I naturally fix on because I've got a big one.'

'And it was talking about your mother being an Olympic swimmer that made me think . . .' She stopped.

'Go on.'

She shook her head. 'It doesn't matter.' She looked at him. 'Your nose isn't so bad. Really.'

He said airily, 'My face I don't mind it, because I am behind it; it's others in front get the view,' and looked at his watch. 'I better go, or Mum'll have my hide.'

It was a relief to have an excuse. *Spooky*, he thought, *queer*, keeping a dead boy's room as he'd left it. Rocking horse, toys, the cuckoo clock still wound up . . . When his grandfather had died in their back bedroom his mother had cleared everything out, his pipes, his clothes – even turned the furniture round so it all looked quite different, ready for Robin to move in, straight after the funeral, out of the room he shared with Sammy and Prue. That had felt odd, he remembered, nothing left of his grandfather, not even the smell of his herbal tobacco, but this was *odder*. Perhaps it seemed odd to Kate, too; perhaps it was what gave her these wafty ideas – everything that belonged to her brother still here and waiting as if he were expected back, as if he might walk in, any minute . . .

Half-way down the stairs, he stopped and looked up. She was standing at the top, arms hugged across her chest as if she were cold.

He said, 'You can come and have tea if you like. Long as you can stand the crush, one more won't make any difference.'

Seaweedy light came through the coloured window and made her face and hands look green. He thought, *Like a mermaid underwater*.

He said, 'I mean, if you're on your own.'

'I'm not. My mother's upstairs, in the studio.'

'That's not what I meant.'

'Oh, I know that!' She smiled, very politely. 'But I don't mind being on my own, thank you all the same. I'm never *lonely*.'

5

'Should have asked her to tea,' Mrs Tite said. 'Since you saw her.'

'Well, I sort of half did,' Robin said. 'But I made a bit of a boob. I said, if you're lonely.'

'Not surprised she didn't come then, no one cares to be pitied.' At the head of her table, Mrs Tite poured tea from a fat, brown pot; her family, who had polished off an enormous lunch only three hours before, tucked in to ham and salad, three kinds of sandwiches and six kinds of cake, as if they had not eaten for weeks.

'Feeding the five thousand, Mother?' Mr Tite, who was a delicate eater, made this remark at every Sunday tea and his wife replied, as she always did, 'People have to keep their strength up, Rome wasn't built on scrag end and parsnips,' and passed him his special plate of thin bread and butter.

'I didn't actually *say* that,' Robin said. 'But she knew what I meant.'

'I'm glad she didn't come.' Prue spoke through a mouthful of ham sandwich. 'I don't like Kate. She's a horrible pig and she's *fat*.'

'That's enough!' Mrs Tite looked at her daughter and Prue looked back at her. Both pairs of eyes were clear as green glass; they met for a long moment and it was Prue's that fell. 'Being rude *and* your mouth full,' Mrs Tite said, calmly enough, but she gave the tiniest of sighs and her husband winked at Robin across the table. *Head on collision any day now*, was what the wink said. Mrs Tite was easy going with her sons because she thought men were really rather unimportant, poor weak creatures to be indulged and petted, but she expected immediate obedience from her daughters. She had always had it from Emerald, her eldest, who was gentle and placid by nature, but she would not get it from Prue, at least not for much longer . . .

Now she muttered, 'She is a pig, then,' but very low, hardly more than a growl in her throat.

Her mother's eyes flashed. '*What* was that?'

'Just she's sorry, I think,' said Emerald, the peacemaker. Big as her mother but softer, cushiony curves instead of solid muscle, she sat comfortably smiling, her baby on her lap. 'Can I have another cup of tea, Mum? If the pot'll stand it.'

'Not this pot won't. I'll make fresh.' Mrs Tite rose with a grunt and went out to the kitchen.

Prue kicked Robin under the table. She said, with her eyes on the door, 'She scared Squib away, being *bossy*. He'll be scared to come back now, case she's there.'

'Give over, can't you?' Robin said.

But Prue was angry. Too little, still, to face up to her mother, she wanted a fight with someone. 'Oh you don't care,' she said. 'He's not *your friend*. If he was your friend it'ud be different, wouldn't it?'

Robin didn't answer. She kicked him again and belched loudly: this was one sure way to annoy him.

He said sharply, 'Don't do that.'

'I can't help it. I got air inside me.'

'Keep it to yourself, then.'

'I can't.'

'Yes you can.'

'I *can't*. You get air inside you, it has to come out, that's Nature. If I tried to keep it back, I might *die*.'

'Perhaps we'd all rather you took the chance!'

Prue stared at him, turning slowly scarlet.

Emerald said, 'Prue, look at Baby! He's eaten a whole egg sandwich, isn't he clever?'

'Finished the plate,' Robin said. He picked it up and followed his mother.

She was standing by the stove. She said, 'Prue over it yet?'

'Started on me. Belching and rudery. So I left her to Emerald.'

Mrs Tite smiled. 'I filled the kettle with cold water. That'll give her time to settle, don't want the sparks to fly on a Sunday, it upsets your father. What's she got against Kate?'

'Nothing, really.' He lingered. 'What did happen, Mum? I mean, to her brother?'

'Drowned.' Mrs Tite lowered her voice to speak of the dead. 'One summer holiday.'

'At the *seaside*?' It was hard for any young Tite to believe. When they swam in the sea their mother was always beside them; a floating tank, a human lifebelt.

'Accidents happen,' Mrs Tite said.

'How did this one?'

Mrs Tite sighed. 'I only know what she's told me. Mr Pollack was out on the raft, sunning himself. She was in a deck-chair, half asleep . . .' She stopped and sighed again.

'Go on,' Robin said.

'Well. One minute the children were there, the next, she looked up and they were both in the sea. The little boy was in a rubber ring but Kate had started to shout and go under. She called out, of course, and her husband dived in, but what could he do? He went for Kate first – she could swim but she'd panicked, out of her depth, and I suppose the boy seemed safe enough in the ring. But he didn't realize the tide had turned. Time he'd got Kate back to the beach the other one was drifting out fast. Bobbing along like a duck, his mother said, a little yellow duck, on the water. His father reached him all right but by then he was out past the raft where the current was strong. It swept them both past the point and she had to stand and watch, poor soul, she couldn't swim and no one else was near . . .'

Robin felt sick. He said, 'Poor Kate. I mean, she must think it was her fault!'

His mother looked at him. 'Not everyone's as tender as you. Besides, I don't suppose she understood it was her or him. A child that age.'

'Prue would know. She's not eight yet.'

'People are different. Mrs Pollack's a sensible woman. I dare say she's told Kate something suitable and Kate's listened. Prue wouldn't listen to God Almighty if he took the trouble to come down to earth and tell her a thing or two!' The kettle began to hum, first one note then another, blending in. Mrs Tite warmed the pot.

Robin said, 'I don't think it's so sensible leaving his room like that, all his toys and things. Like a sort of *shrine*.'

'I wouldn't say it was like that.' Mrs Tite measured tea, poured water, eyes screwed up against the steam. 'More like she just never bothered. Why should she, the house is big enough? And she had other things to think about, earning a living for one thing, so she just shut the doors and carried on.'

'I don't think it was like that. I mean, it doesn't feel like that,' Robin said obstinately. But he didn't know how it did feel. Whether it was the room, or just Kate, that seemed strange to him. He would have liked to say, *Kate thinks he's still alive*, but it was not the sort of thing he could say to his mother.

Instead he said, 'Why didn't Mrs Pollack sell the house when they died? I mean, it's so huge, just for two.'

'Don't suppose she felt like it. They'd only bought it, couple of months before. I helped her move in, I couldn't do much, Sam was only a baby, but she's the sort makes you want to be useful. Such a little thing, thin as a lath and all eyes. I said, "What d'you want a great old place like this for?" and she said, "Oh, we want space, Mrs Tite, we're going to have a big family, three boys and three girls." ' Mrs Tite stopped. Her expression was unnaturally soft. She said, 'Well, you have to take what the Lord sends, in this hard old life.'

'That sounds a bit meek for you, Mother,' Emerald said, in

34

the doorway. 'Dad says, where's that tea? Prue and Sammy are bored, they want to get down.'

'Not till other people have finished, they know the rules.' Mrs Tite picked up the pot and moved swiftly, but Emerald stood in her way.

She said gently, 'Prue did ask, Mum, and Dad said they could. They wanted to go to the park and Dad said it's the best place, this hot weather.'

The two big women filled the kitchen. The baby in Emerald's arms gurgled and tugged his mother's hair over her eyes and Mrs Tite smiled. 'I thought they were scared on their own. That lonely old path.'

'I expect it's worn off,' Robin said. 'Or they want to go more.'

Emerald pushed her hair back. She said, 'I think they've gone to look for someone,' and kissed her baby's fat neck.

6

'I DON'T want to,' Sammy said.

'Cowardy custard.' But Prue was uncertain herself. They stood on the path and looked through the broken fence into Turner's Wood. A few shafts of sunlight filtered down through the trees, but it was mostly dark; dark green and secret.

Sammy said, 'Suppose he's there? Suppose he jumps out?'

'He won't. He didn't before. He only turned nasty when we teased him.'

Sammy still hung back. Prue said, 'Don't you want to find Squib?'

Sammy sighed, very deeply.

Prue jerked his arm. 'It was you said he lived there, you said he told you. Was that a *lie*?'

Sammy shook his head.

'Cross your heart?'

He licked his forefinger and drew it across his throat. His eyes were big. He said, 'Suppose the witch catches us and puts *us* in the basket and fattens us up to eat?'

'*That's* not true. Not the witch part.' But Prue hesitated. She might not listen to most people, but she listened to Sammy. Though he was smaller and weaker in every other way, his imagination was stronger; his tales became true in the telling. And the wood did look very dark.

Sammy said fearfully, 'It's a chanted wood. A chanted wood round a castle.'

'*En*chanted, silly. And it's not a castle, just the Old People's Home.' Prue felt suddenly bolder. She said, 'Oh, come on . . .'

Sammy had no choice: she held him by the wrist. Through the fence and into the wood – quite a long way into it, in her first, determined rush. He stumbled after her, through tangly undergrowth that plucked his clothes and scratched his ankles. He thought he saw dark shapes out of the corners of his eyes. He said, 'Prue . . .' and sobbed in his throat.

She stopped so abruptly that he bumped into her. She said sternly, 'All right then, go back. Go back by yourself.'

He pressed closer. 'I heard something.' They listened. There were small sounds all round them; leaves rustling, twigs cracking. The wood was alive . . . 'Squirrels', Prue said, 'birds' and, as if to answer her, a pigeon bubbled up aloft.

'There you are,' she said.

He clutched her hand. 'Suppose she's eaten him already.'

Prue felt cold. His round, pink face was so solemn, his voice so hushed. She whispered back, 'He couldn't have got fat enough in just *two days*.' Then she gave a high, excited laugh. 'Don't be a *nit*, Sam Tite, we're only going to ask if he can come out. Just call for him, you are *silly*.'

He sighed, a little, quivery sigh. He still held her hand, but more loosely. He said, 'Look, there's a path.'

It was overgrown and soggy under their feet. They followed it past what had once been a big kitchen garden: an old fruit cage with the netting in holes, several green houses with rotting frames and most of the glass broken. Only one shed still seemed used: there were tools inside in neat rows and a wheelbarrow at the door, full of rose prunings. Then the path twisted and broadened and they walked on firmer ground, between bushes of speckled laurel, until it opened out altogether, on to the gardens of Turner's Tower.

Lawns, flower beds where tulips grew in rows like marshalled soldiers, a gravel walk with wooden seats. Some of the old people sat there, wrapped in rugs in spite of the hot sun; others crept up and down the paved terrace beneath the high walls of the house that was built like a castle, with battlements and narrow, pointed windows.

The children stood indecisively. 'He don't live in the House, he lives in the Tower,' Sammy said.

The Tower stood to the right of the house and was shaded by it; a tall, round building on which no sun fell. Except for the birds flying and twittering in and out of the ivy it seemed untenanted: the wooden door at the bottom was closed and the uncurtained windows looked like blind eyes. Like a prison, Prue thought. She was frightened of prisons, of being locked up in the dark . . .

'No one lives there,' she said.

'Squib does.'

'You ask then.'

Poked from behind, Sammy went forward reluctantly. None of the old people looked dangerous, even if some of them seemed dead, sitting there corpse-pale in the sun, their papery eyelids closed. One was alive, though; a short, stout lady whose eyes were open and watching them. As they came near, she smiled with one side of her mouth.

Sammy said, 'Please, Miss . . .' and stopped.

She spoke out of one side of her mouth, too. 'What do you want?' She touched the hearing aid on her chest and it whistled. 'Speak up now,' she said.

The flesh hung from the bones of her face in powdery pouches, a small one from each cheek and several bigger ones from her chin. She was almost bald; the little hair she had left was orange-coloured and soft as cotton wool.

Sammy was so fascinated he couldn't speak. He simply stared, his nostrils pinching in and out. Prue nudged him to remind him of his manners and said, with her best smile but a beating heart, 'We're looking for our friend.'

'Must be over ninety if he lives here. What's his name?'

The children looked at each other. Prue said uncertainly, 'He's just a boy we play with. A little boy. We're looking for him.'

The old lady laughed; a wheezy sound like a pair of dusty

bellows. 'You'd better look somewhere else then. No children here, not allowed. This is a rest home for old horses.' She laughed again and her chin pouches shook like jelly bags. 'Out to grass,' she said. 'Next stop the knacker's yard.'

Sammy slipped his hand into Prue's.

The old lady took a lace handkerchief out of the neck of her blouse and wiped her mouth. 'All we're fit for, cat meat. But you had better watch out. Nice young plump things like you. No dogs, no children, that's Matron's rule. She catches you, she'll have your lights and livers.'

Sammy tugged at Prue's hand.

'Put you in a pie soon as look at you,' the old lady said. 'Four and twenty blackbirds, you know the song?'

Prue nodded. She began to walk slowly backwards.

'When the pie was opened, the birds began to sing, wasn't that a dainty dish to set before a king?' The old lady sang in a cracked, piping voice, beating time with one hand.

'Come away,' Sammy whispered. 'Oh Prue, come away.'

They backed, hands tightly clasped; then turned and flew for the path. Fear grew as they ran; by the time they reached the shelter of the laurels, red lights were dancing in front of their eyes and their hearts were pumping so hard they could scarcely breathe. Sammy said, through chattering teeth, 'I told you she'd eat him, I *told* you.'

Prue put her arms round him. 'She's mad, crazy mad,' she said, but she was, in a way, more frightened than Sammy. He had her to comfort him; she had no one. She wanted her mother. She said, 'Let's go home quick.'

They ran, on rubbery legs. The wood seemed a friendly place now, with this horror behind them. But their path was blocked: as they turned, by the shed, someone stood in their way.

He was a tall, thin boy with a great mop of dry, frizzy hair. Sammy, who was leading, cannoned straight into his stomach;

the boy grunted, and caught him. 'Hey, what's the hurry?' he said.

Sammy looked up into his face and gasped. The boy said, 'I know *you* . . .'

Sammy flung himself at Prue. She pushed him behind her and said in a shrill voice, 'Don't you scare him again with that knife, don't you *dare*. My Dad's a policeman, I told him of you an' he said, you scare him again an' he'll catch you and put you in prison.'

'I know your Dad,' the boy said. 'He works down the Supermarket, on the meat counter.' He looked at Prue and laughed suddenly. 'S'all right, I won't eat you. Least, not today.'

Sammy burst into tears. He sobbed, 'I don't want to be put in a pie.'

The boy looked astonished. 'Hey,' he said. 'What's up?' and then, when Sammy went on howling, eyes screwed up so tight that the water spurted out sideways, 'Here, have a fag.' He fumbled in his pocket.

Sammy opened his eyes. The boy lit a squashed cigarette, drew on it till it flared, and offered it to Sammy. Sammy's chest still heaved but he had stopped crying. 'Go on,' the boy said.

Sammy went bright pink. He took the cigarette.

'Draw it in, t'wont kill you,' the boy said.

Sammy inhaled, turned pinker still, and began to cough.

'Steady on, you got to get accustomed,' the boy said. 'Best to sit down the first time.'

He took him just inside the shed and sat him on a plank. Then he turned to Prue. 'Take his mind off for a minute,' he said. 'What was that bawling for?'

Prue looked at him. When they had teased him that day, following him up the path and shouting, *Wild One, Wild One, Silly Old Wild One*, until he had lost his temper and threatened them with his knife, he had seemed quite terrifying: six feet tall and savage. Now she saw he had a nice face, if a bit thin and dirty. She said, 'What you said about eating. He says there's a witch up at the Tower eats little boys.'

He started to laugh, then pulled his face straight. He said, 'Oh, you're all right today. Today's Sunday. She don't eat people Sundays, only Tuesdays and Thursdays.'

Prue thought he was joking but she couldn't be sure. She had hoped he would say, 'What rubbish.' Now she didn't know what to believe. Fear dragged at her stomach. She scowled and said, 'We ought to go home now. Come on, Sammy.'

He staggered out of the shed. His face wasn't pink any more, but yellow as a daffodil. 'I feel sick,' he said. And was – into a clump of nettles.

'You have to get used to it,' the boy said, wiping him down with a rag from the tool shed.

Sammy's mouth turned down. 'I want my Mum.'

'Don't tell her what you've bin up to, then! Smoking! A kid your age!' The boy cuffed him on the side of the head, very gently, and winked at Prue.

She wished he had given her a cigarette. *She* wouldn't have been sick. She said, 'We saw you down the park yesterday. With your gang.'

He shook his head. 'Not yesterday you didn't. I got chucked out last week 'cause me bike's broke.'

'How *mean*,' Prue said. 'I think that's really mean!'

He shrugged his thin shoulders. '*I* don't care, do I? Lot of silly kids.'

Sammy said, 'It still says *The Wild One* on the back of your jacket.'

'Paint won't come off, will it? Got to save up, buy a new one.'

Prue said, 'Do you work here?'

'Gardener's boy. Five poun' a week and me dinner.'

She said, importantly, 'My brother's going to be a teacher!'

'Grammar school yob.' He leaned against the door of the shed and yawned till his jaw cracked.

Prue giggled. She thought he was so funny and nice. That was a good name to call Robin! She said, 'We've got to go now, but we'll come back if you like.'

'I don't mind.' He yawned and stretched. Then he said, 'Better not tell your Mum, though.'

'She won't mind.'

'Oh, won't she?' He looked at Prue for a minute, rather shyly. Then he grinned and shook his mop of hair forward. 'Well, you suit yourself, but I warn you, t'isn't safe, spreading tales. Not with that old cannibal up at the Tower! She gets to hear there's a couple of little kids nosing round, it might put her in mind of her stomach!'

The children looked at each other and drew closer together until their hands were touching.

'Oh, we won't tell anyone, we *never* tell people things,' Sammy said.

7

'I CAN'T get anything out of them,' Robin said. 'They just look at each other and giggle.'

A bit odd, he had thought. They had always talked about Squib before. Now all this week, they hadn't mentioned him once. Not since last Sunday.

'Get them separately,' Kate said.

'I tried. Not Sam, he'd just make up something weird and wonderful, but I asked Prue. Did she have any idea where he lived, what did she really know about his Auntie, that sort of thing. But she clammed up, went sort of *blank*. Almost as if she didn't know who I was talking about.'

Or was hiding something. Not just from him, from herself. Stubborn little face, solid as a cold rice pudding, but a look in her eyes, a bit sly, a bit scared. As if something had frightened her and she'd shut it away, locked some door in her mind. Better not tell Kate *that*, Robin thought.

He said, 'Perhaps they've just lost interest. Since he hasn't been back. You know what kids are.'

That was more like it! Prue had simply been bored! He had talked about Squib but she hadn't been listening. She had said, 'What's a cannibal, Robin?'

Kate said, 'I've been down to the park every afternoon straight after school. He always used to be there.'

She looked desolate and not very well. There were smudges under her eyes and a hint of tears in them; she bent over Hugo's pram and fussed with the covers. Robin watched her, swinging on his front gate. He said, 'You feeling all right?'

'Bit of a belly ache.' She straightened up. 'He can't just have vanished off the face of the earth.'

For some reason this had a sinister ring. The tone of her voice, perhaps.

Robin said, 'Look – people vanish every day but not off the earth, just we don't happen to see them again. They've moved, or changed their habits, or something.'

'I'm frightened,' she said.

'What of?'

'I don't know.'

But she did. She smiled fixedly at Hugo who was chewing his rattle and dribbling.

Robin said, 'I won't laugh.'

She glanced at him quickly, then back to Hugo again. She said in a low voice, 'It's just I keep thinking. It's since I recognized him. As if he'd been waiting for that, and soon as I did he went away.'

Robin had no desire to laugh at all. He said, 'Do you believe that?'

'Yes. No. I don't *know* . . .' She wriggled her shoulders and sighed.

'You mean, like a ghost, or something?' This was a funny conversation to be having in broad daylight – Saturday afternoon with people out washing their cars or cutting the grass.

She said, 'I don't know. I keep dreaming. Then I wake up and it's all confused. I can't explain.'

'What's in the dream?'

'Different things. He's running away through a wood and it's dangerous, but I have to go after him. And sometimes I can see him and sometimes I can't, but I can hear him crying. And sometimes he's drowning . . .'

This made some sense and he seized on it thankfully. 'In the sea?'

'No. A sort of lake, deep and dark. Not like anywhere I've ever been. Black water . . .' The colour came and went in her face and she shivered.

He laughed, rather awkwardly. 'You'll have me scared in a

45

minute.' She had certainly scared herself. Or perhaps she was sickening for something. He said, 'You've got yourself into a proper old state, haven't you? You look awful.'

'I feel awful. All the time. Mixed up in my stomach and mixed up in my head.'

He didn't know how to reply to that. To hide his embarrassment, he swung on the gate, lifting his feet backwards and hanging from his armpits.

She said, 'I don't know what to do,' and smiled at him timidly. 'I better take Hugo in, I suppose. Time for his tea.'

She wheeled the pram into the next-door garden. Her departing back looked hunched and sad.

Robin knew he had let her down. He stayed where he was for a while, swinging, and pulling faces to distract himself from this uncomfortable feeling. Then he got down, kicked the gate shut, and went indoors.

His mother was ironing. Thump, *thump* – as if she were punishing something. The warm, steamy smell filled the kitchen. Robin stood by the table.

She said, 'Fine spectator sport, watching other people work. You want a job?'

'No, thanks. I've got homework left. Latin.' He smiled at the thought: he always left Latin to the last for the pleasure of looking forward to it, the way the little ones kept the best bit of food on their plates till the end of the meal. He said, 'Old Squeaky-boots says I can start Greek next term, if I go on as I'm going.'

Mrs Tite folded a shirt and pressed it flat, wiggling the point of the iron between the buttons. 'You know what your father'll say. Science, not Classics. You know that.'

Robin's heart thumped. 'Back me up, Mum.'

'You need backing, then you don't want it much.' She spread one of Prue's frocks on the board and held the iron near her cheek, to test it. 'Greek. What's the use?'

'It opens doors,' Robin said, not knowing how else to put it.

Then he thought of a better thing to say to his mother. 'What's the use of anything, come to that? What's the use of swimming further and faster than the next person?'

'It was all I wanted to do at one time, where'd it get me?'

'That doesn't matter, does it?'

The big woman looked at him, a bit grim and thoughtful. 'I'm not educated, nor is your father. He's got the brains, he'll read till his eyes drop out, but that's not the same thing. You've got chances, it's important you pick the right ones.'

'I want to learn Greek,' Robin said. 'It's all I want to do.'

His mother smiled suddenly as if this was the answer she had been waiting for. 'Tell your father that, then, don't hide behind me.' She spat on the cooling iron and started on Prue's dress. Robin stayed, perched on the edge of the table. She said, after a minute, 'Well, Professor? What else d'you want to say?'

He was startled; his mother often startled him, the way she came out with things she hadn't been told. It was as if she had a spare eye somewhere, that saw into your mind.

He said, 'Nothing, really. Just about Kate.'

Mrs Tite finished the dress and stretched up to hang it over the airer. Her bare arms were smooth and freckled. She said, 'You quarrelled, or something?'

Robin shook his head. 'It's just she's acting funny.'

'What d'you mean?'

'I don't know.' He couldn't imagine what he had thought he might say. *She's seeing ghosts? She's going mad?* He said, 'Oh, forget it,' slid off the table and made for the back door.

Mrs Tite said, 'Maybe it's because Sophie's leaving.'

Robin stopped. 'I didn't know.'

'Well, she is. Next week. Not that her ladyship takes me into her confidence in the ordinary way but she wants me to mind the baby when the men come. Not that they've much to move, just a few sticks that would fit on a barrow.'

Robin said slowly, 'I don't think Kate knows. She'd have said.'

47

'Then she's got a shock coming. She'll miss that baby. She's not got much, poor child.'

'No brothers or sisters? She doesn't know when she's well off!'

'She's lonely,' his mother said. 'Not that she need be, there's that great house and garden and her mother wouldn't mind who she had in. But she doesn't make friends the way some do.'

'She thinks Sophie's her friend,' Robin said.

8

KATE called, 'Sophie.'

'Here, ducky-love.'

Kate carried Hugo into the living-room. The only furnishing was an old leather sofa with a book under one leg to keep it level, and a new, pearl-grey carpet. Sophie was sitting on the floor, painting her toe-nails raspberry colour. She said, 'Back already?'

'It's so hot out,' Kate said. Hugo felt very heavy. 'Shall I put him down?'

'Not on the carpet, sweet. I expect his behind is sopping. Besides, my nails aren't dry yet. Could you be a *lamb* and give him his tea?'

Kate sighed, but only a little, and went into the kitchen. She put Hugo in the playpen and gave him a bread crust to chew while she warmed his bottle. Apart from milk, there wasn't much in the refrigerator: a packet of frozen peas, a few curling rashers of bacon, a half empty tin of sardines. Kate wondered if Sophie was terribly poor in spite of her red sports car and Hugo's new pram, and thought how marvellous it would be if she could send her a hundred pounds in a parcel. She wouldn't put her name, of course, just From a Well-Wisher, or An Anonymous Friend. Or if she could creep in one day before she was awake with a great basket of food: chicken and peaches and a Fuller's coffee cream cake. Sophie would come down in the dressing-gown she wore in the mornings, short and frilled and polka-dotted, and when she saw the feast set out her eyes would fill with happy tears. 'Darling,' she would call to her husband, 'darling, we've had a *visitation*. Our Good Fairy . . .'

But it was difficult to imagine Sophie saying anything quite like this and Kate felt too heavy and dull to invent anything more likely. The pain that had been coming and going all afternoon seemed to be permanent now, fixed and solid like a lead ball in her stomach. And her head hurt: when Hugo threw his crust away and began to cry, little men with hobnailed boots stamped about inside her skull. She picked him up to give him his bottle and he quietened at once, sucking away with half-closed eyes. This was usually one of the best times, sitting with Hugo warm and contented on her lap, but today he felt simply heavy, a heavy lump of damp, greedy baby, and her arms ached holding him.

Sophie came into the kitchen, walking on her heels. Her feet were still bare and there were little pads of cotton wool between her toes to keep the nails separate.

She said, 'I had to give them another coat. Would you be an absolute *saint* and *angel* and bathe him for me?'

'I feel so sick,' Kate said.

'Sick?' Sophie smiled, a bit crossly. 'Too much ice-cream?'

Kate shuddered. Even the word *ice-cream* made her stomach heave. She longed to lie down on the cold, kitchen floor, but she was still holding Hugo. She said, 'I'm sorry,' and Sophie bent over her and gathered him up.

She said, 'Well, you'd better go home if you're ill, hadn't you?'

Kate felt she was going to cry. She pulled her face about to stop herself and stood up.

Standing, she managed to smile. 'I'm so sorry, Sophie.'

'I expect it'll pass off. If not, we'll bring fruit and flowers to your sick bed, won't we, Hugo-baby? A *cornucopia*!' She jiggled him up and down and a little milk leaked out of the corner of his mouth. Over his head, Sophie looked at Kate and said, more kindly, 'You do look a bit rotten. All right to go home by yourself, Katey-ducky?'

'Oh, of course, I'm fine really,' Kate said. 'Thank you, Sophie.'

But crossing the road was an ordeal: the sun struck painfully white, and cars were black shadows, zipping past. Once inside the house, in the sea-green cool of the hall, she felt better, perhaps because safer: it would have been dreadful to be sick in public. She was sick in the bathroom, pulled the plug and rinsed her mouth and came out on to the landing. No sound – then a tiny, tinny whirring, and a clock struck. Cuckoo, cuckoo . . . The door of Rupert's room was ajar. Perhaps she had left it like that; her mother never went in there.

Kate closed it quietly. Then she thought, suddenly, *Perhaps he was a ghost like Robin said. Not a boy, not a changeling, but the ghost of Rupert, come back . . .*

She stood on the silent landing and her mind began to whirl; thoughts seemed to dance in it, zig-zag and aimless, like midges. *My brother, so my ghost – The others only saw him because I made them – Prue knows that, it's why she won't talk about him – She knows he was magic . . .*

'Little children understand magic,' her mother had said once. 'It's a gift you lose as you grow older.'

Perhaps *she* was too old, had suddenly become too old, that's why he had gone away.

It made her sad, thinking that. Then the pain grew worse in her stomach, like a knot tightening. She climbed the stairs to find her mother but the studio was empty and Kate remembered that she often went shopping late on Saturday afternoons when the shops were less crowded. It was hot in the studio with the sun blazing in and she pushed the window open. The evening breeze blew cool on her forehead and puffed papers off the table.

She closed the window and went to pick them up. Her mother's rough sketches: drawings of Turner's Wood, tall trees with twisted branches, and drawings of children, playing, running, laughing . . . Some were just faces seen from different angles; Sammy's round, baby face and Prue's, sharper and thinner. A good face, her mother had said. That meant interesting. Kate looked at the drawings carefully, trying to see what her mother saw, and thought she had made Prue look older than she really was in some of them. There was one of her by the gravel pit, down near the river: Kate recognized the background and the notice, Danger, Deep Water. This was a made-up picture, Kate knew: the Tite children were not allowed to play by the river and she had never seen Prue look as frightened as that. She was running away from the pit with her hair flying wild and the gaunt, bare machinery behind her. *What is she running from?* Kate thought, and sighed. She wished she could draw, not because she wanted to, for herself, but because they expected it at school. 'You don't take after your clever mother, do you?' the art mistress said. Rupert had taken after her, he had been clever; he couldn't draw, but he could read and do sums. At four years old he had doubled numbers in his head for pleasure. Kate remembered her mother saying, 'We think Rupert is really quite exceptional.' And, perhaps the same occasion, perhaps not, 'I'm afraid Kate's talents are purely domestic.' *Why afraid?* Kate thought.

She sighed again and shuffled the drawings. There were several of her, some she had posed for, others her mother had done when she wasn't looking. Prettier than Prue, a softer face. 'Not interesting, though,' Kate said, and put them at the bottom of the pile.

There was a picture of Robin, beaky nose and foxy grin. And on the same sheet, one of Squib. Only head and shoulders, but it was him to the life!

Kate stared at it. She felt dizzy and confused but excitement seemed to beat through her head, like music. He wasn't a ghost, then! You couldn't draw a ghost, only out of your mind, and her mother never worked from imagination. She must have done this the day she came down to the park. She was too old to see ghosts. Since she had seen him, he was *real* . . .

She thought, *I must tell Robin.* She put the other drawings tidily on the table with a glass paperweight on top, and started down the stairs. On the landing the pain began again, so bad that she had to bend over; she waited, counting under her breath until it eased a little. Counting was a good thing if something was hurting you; reciting poetry even better. She tried, *So all day long the noise of battle rolled among the mountains by the winter sea,* and it got her out of the house and across the road before the pain came back, like an iron hand clutching.

She pushed open Robin's gate, doubled up and gasping. No sign of him; only Sammy, sitting in a cardboard box and waving two pieces of wood. She said, 'Hallo, Sam,' but his face was set and fierce and he didn't answer her: the box was a boat he was rowing across the stormy Atlantic.

The short front path was miles long; she knocked on the door and it was a hundred years before anyone opened it. And then it wasn't Robin.

She said, 'Mrs Tite, is Robin in?' But it wasn't Mrs Tite.

Emerald said, 'He's doing his homework. Kate dear, what's wrong?'

She felt sweat on her forehead like melting ice. She said, 'Emerald, I'm going to die,' and pitched forward.

Emerald caught her. She said, 'Not yet, I hope,' picked her up like one of her own babies, and carried her indoors.

9

Robin said, 'Is she all right, Mum?'

Sunday morning sun slanted through the window. The big bed almost filled the small room and Mrs Tite filled the bed; a mountain under blankets. Beside her Mr Tite slept neatly and inconspicuously, taking up very little space and barely lifting the bedclothes.

Mrs Tite said, 'Wake up, Father. Robin's brought the tea.' And then, heaving herself with sighs and grunts into a sitting position, 'Right as rain *now*. They took her appendix out. I looked in to tell you last night but you were out like a light.'

'I tried to keep awake,' Robin said. 'I waited and waited.'

Mrs Tite blew gently on her steaming cup. Her face was the colour of a foxglove and puffy with sleep. 'Her poor Mum didn't come back till getting on for midnight. She'd stayed at the hospital till it was all over. Poor soul, she was so upset, blaming herself for not being here, for not noticing the child was ill, for everything under the sun! Even for working so hard! 'I don't need to,' she said, 'it's become like a drug to me.' Well, you can't do everything, I told her, be mother and father both, and all's well that ends well.' She sipped her tea and looked at Robin. 'You said Kate had been acting funny, didn't you? Well, I dare say this has been blowing up for some time, that's what's been wrong with her.'

'It'll do to be going on with,' Robin said. 'Give Dad a poke or his tea will be cold.'

He clattered down the stairs and out into the sparkling air. Days like this he enjoyed the newspaper round; the world to himself and birds singing. He whistled as he swung on his bike and went down the path; sunlight, shifting through trees, made his eyes dazzle. No one about, not on the path, nor in the town. The main street slept in the sun that was so warm already that the newsagent's dog was stretched out on the step as if in the heat of the day. He looked like a dead dog until Robin stepped over him and saw his skin ripple and twitch as he dreamed hunting dreams in his sleep.

'Good to be alive, morning like this,' the newsagent said.

Robin wondered if Kate was awake and thinking that. She had said, *Emerald, I'm going to die,* and Robin, standing at the top of the stairs, had felt his stomach lurch as if he had looked down a precipice. Then Emerald was carrying her in; he had seen her white face and her hair, dark and wet as if she'd been drowning . . .

'Best part of the day,' the newsagent said. 'Bound to cloud over later.'

No sign of cloud now. Only blue, clear blue that made your eyes ache looking at it.

Bound to be awake, Robin thought. They woke you early in hospital with a clatter of trolleys. He had only been in hospital once, the time he had come off his bike and gone in for X-rays and to have his head stitched, and he had rather enjoyed it; being important and fussed over. But he hadn't been scared and in pain, just a bang when the car hit his wheel and then waking in bed with a pretty nurse telling him to lie still. Not like Kate, who'd had to wait for what must have seemed hours before the ambulance came, doubled up and moaning and afraid of dying. He had sat on the stairs listening until Emerald came out and sent him away. 'Run along, love. Mother's gone for the doctor, if you want to help, keep the little ones out in the garden.' He had said, 'What's she saying? Will she *die*?' – hardly able to get the words out, his tongue seemed so swollen and thick in his mouth, and Emerald had smiled to comfort him, though he could see her forehead creased with worry. 'Goodness me no – she sounds worse than she is, muttering on about ghosts and a lot of old nonsense, but it's only the fever.'

He had nearly cried out, 'It's not nonsense, she has seen a ghost!' but stopped himself in time. Emerald was kind and gentle and good but she was not someone you could say this kind of thing to. Like her mother, like Robin, really, she only believed in what she could see and touch.

Now, delivering newspapers this clean, sunny morning, he felt sick with relief that he hadn't said it, hadn't made such a fool of himself. Ghosts indeed! He would never have heard the last of it!

He gave a sudden, embarrassed laugh, hurled a tied bundle of newspapers on to a porch and then glanced up at the windows; this sort of house, they expected their newspapers put through the letter box and made a fuss if they weren't. But there was no sign of life and Robin put his thumb to his nose. 'Want to make something of it?' he said aloud and cycled fast out of the drive, head down. A winding road, all uphill; big houses set wide apart. 'Three cars in the garage and lousy tips,' Robin said, standing on his pedals to get up the rise and turning, at the top, into a shorter, straighter street: smaller houses, built in pairs, like Siamese twins. Smaller houses, poorer people, but they gave better tips, didn't yell the place down if you took a short cut across a bit of grass, didn't complain if you were late in bad weather. 'Maybe more of them's been delivery boys, the others don't know what it's like,' was what Mrs Tite said. 'Even rich people can think, can't they?' Robin answered her now, holding this grumbling conversation inside his head, 'Rotten, tight-wad lot' – though it wasn't the tips he minded really, more the feeling that he didn't exist for those sort of people. He was just the newspaper boy . . .

No tips at Turner's Tower, except for an old lady who gave him one of her dead husband's handkerchiefs every Christmas – A for Arthur, or Archibald, embroidered in one corner – but Robin didn't mind that. They were old and on pension and they smiled if they saw him and called him by his name.

When he arrived this morning, Colonel Wittering was sitting on the terrace, eyes blinkered like an owl's in the sun, hands clasped over the pearl top of his walking stick. Old hands with veins like tender, blue ropes and a thick nose with a divided, red blob at the tip. Ex-Indian Army, retired for more years than Robin had lived. He said, 'Morning, Robin, always the early bird,' and laughed, showing jagged, mustard-yellow teeth with a flash of gold at the back. *Always be polite to the natives*, Robin thought, but he liked the Colonel and grinned at his joke as he gave him his *Sunday Times*, neatly folded. The rest of the papers he spread out fan-wise on the long table in the entrance hall; a gloomy place, dark as winter and hung with the moth-eaten heads of dead deer. Robin felt the chill in his bones and was glad to get out again. Hate to live here, he thought, though he wouldn't mind the house-keeper's Tower which was romantic and ivy-draped, a private eyrie . . .

He left her *Express* on the mounting block by the stable door. There had once been horses kept here; the round rooms above the old stable were reached by a wooden stair. A good place, Robin thought, secret and peaceful. You could live there shut away from the world; a hermit or an eccentric Professor, reading Greek in the daytime and going abroad at night, sweeping through dark streets in a big, black cloak. He stood back from the Tower, looked up – and saw Squib at the window.

There was no doubt. A smudge of pale face, pale hair. And yet, the next minute, he wondered. Just that one glimpse and he'd gone. Robin stood still, craning upwards and watching, but the window was a dark eye, staring out. He thought, *Don't be silly, you saw him! You're not that nutty yet! No mystery after all, just the housekeeper's boy* . . .

He could have laughed out loud. Until then, he didn't realize how uncomfortable he'd been. Caught up in that daft girl's imaginings . . . He inhaled deeply as if he felt suddenly

short of air and said, 'You want your head examined, Robin Tite.'

He turned to wheel his bike away and stopped. The top half of the stable door was a little ajar and someone was coming down the stairs inside. Not Squib, not any child. Too slow. Flip-flop, like a woman in soft slippers. He bent over the handlebars, pretending to be rearranging the bag so it wouldn't catch on the front wheel, and she pushed open the door. Presumably Matron got breakfast Sunday mornings and she was off duty; she wore a Japanese kimono as a dressing-gown, big sleeves fluttering like coloured wings as she bent to pick up her paper. Dyed hair, yellow as buttercups but dark at the roots; a flat face like a plate with features painted on. No teeth in yet: when she saw Robin one hand went up to her mouth and she looked at him over it.

He said cheerily, 'Lovely morning,' and thought, *Better make sure*. Check and double check, his Latin master advised. He said, 'I meant to ask Friday but I didn't see you. I had a comic left over, was it yours?'

'Mine?' She laughed, still keeping her hand up but pretending to rub an itch on her nose with the back of it. The eyes above were so blank they might really have been painted, and by a bad painter; they had no depth, no shine.

'Well, not for you, I didn't mean. For the boy.'

'What boy?'

This came out sharp as gunfire and made Robin jump. He said, 'Oh,' and looked up. 'Well. Him . . .'

'There's only me lives here.' She lifted her chin, looking incredulous. Red patches appeared on her cheek-bones. 'I'm sure I don't know what you're talking about.'

Too emphatic, Robin thought; protesting too much. If she really didn't know, she'd have just shrugged her shoulders, taken her paper and gone in to read it over a cup of tea instead of standing there and glaring at him as if he'd insulted her.

She said, 'What are you up to, anyway? Hanging around, poking your nose in.'

He said, 'I'm not, I just asked. I made a mistake, didn't I?' and she took a hold on herself visibly, taking her hand from her face to draw her kimono together and smiling at him with a closed mouth.

She said, 'All right. Didn't mean to bite your head off, no offence meant.' And then, still trying to be amiable but not quite managing it, 'Keep off the grass now, with that bike.'

He didn't reply to this, but turned his back. He heard the bottom half of the door close, then the top; clicked into place and bolted. He walked away wheeling the bike and wondering what she thought she was up to. She'd got him there all right, got him hidden, but why? No answer he could think of, unless she'd kidnapped him or something ...

He thought, *kidnapped*, and whistled through his teeth. Then he saw someone was watching from the far side of the lawn, near the bushes: a tall, thin boy, wearing a black jacket and carrying a bucket. Robin put his bike down on the path and as he crossed the grass the boy seemed to shrink back, as if he had meant to keep out of sight.

Robin said, 'Who lives in the Tower?'

The boy put the bucket down and flexed his fingers nervously. His light blue eyes flickered. A bit vacant, Robin thought, a screw loose, but no harm in asking.

He said, 'Apart from the housekeeper, I mean,' and went closer. Too close: the boy quivered like a startled, wild creature and bent for the bucket. Robin saw the name painted on the back of his jacket and it drove everything else out of his mind.

He said, 'I know who you are! Scaring little kids! You're lucky we didn't go to the police!'

The boy didn't speak. After one quick, frightened glance, he turned his head away and stood still.

Robin took hold of his arm. He could feel it trembling through the leather sleeve and the boy's fear excited him. He said, 'You rotten, stinking bully, you do it again and I'll bash you up good and proper.' He shook him, for emphasis, and the boy twisted suddenly, like an eel. He said, 'Let go of me,' in a shrill, shaking voice and swiped at Robin's face, knocking his glasses off. Robin shouted with rage and kicked the back of the boy's calf with his heel. They fell on the path, the boy underneath; he drew up his knee and jabbed Robin in the stomach. They rolled over and over, pummelling, scratching; Robin tangled his hand in the thick, frizzy hair and the boy hit him in the throat. Pain, like a sudden flash of darkness; Robin gasped, thumped the boy's head on the gravel and then gasped again as a flood of cold water drenched the back of his head and neck. The shock made him loosen his hold; the boy wriggled free and got to his feet, treading on Robin's hand as he did so. Then he was gone, and Robin sat up, water streaming down his face and soaking his shirt.

'Only way to stop a dog fight that I know of,' Colonel Wittering said, and handed him his glasses.

10

'No visitor this afternoon?' Sister said. 'No *Mummy*?'

'I told her not to bother,' Kate said. 'I'm expecting my friend.'

Over a week had gone by and no Sophie, but Kate hadn't minded: each day she didn't come made it more likely she would come the next. And today was *certain* – she was going home tomorrow and after that it would be too late to come with fruit and flowers . . .

'Better hurry up then,' Sister said. 'Visiting hour's nearly over.'

'Only half over,' Kate said.

She watched the swing doors at the end of the ward. Everyone else had the two visitors they were allowed so the next time the doors opened it was bound to be Sophie. She thought, a watched pot never boils, and looked at the clock at the other end of the ward instead. The clock had a red second hand which moved very slowly; a minute was a long time when you were waiting. Perhaps it was cheating to watch the clock, as bad as watching the doors! Kate lay back on the pillows and shut her eyes tight.

Sister said, 'Here's your visitor, Kate,' and her heart missed a beat. But it was only Robin, standing beside the bed with a silly grin on his face and a bunch of violets in his hand.

He said awkwardly, 'Here you are,' and put them on the locker. They were squashed from being in his pocket.

Kate felt dull and disappointed but she said, 'Thank you,' and then, rather less politely, 'I didn't think *you'd* come.'

'Well, wonders never cease,' Robin said.

She picked up the violets and sniffed. 'They don't smell.'

'Hothouse,' Robin said. 'They never do.'

'Oh. I didn't know that.'

'Well you know now,' Robin said.

The end of that conversation. They looked at each other.

Kate said, 'You can sit on the bed. Sister doesn't mind. And you can have a grape if you like.'

Her mother had brought them last night. They were bloomy black grapes, big as damsons.

Robin tried one. 'Bit sour,' he said, but he took another and then another, as if he couldn't think of anything else to do.

'Go on,' Kate said. 'I don't like grapes much.'

'Shouldn't eat them anyway, not with an appendix,' Robin said. 'Does it hurt?'

'Not now.'

He smiled shyly and put another grape in his mouth. He said, 'It's raining out, cats and dogs. Bed's the best place.'

'Not when you have to be in it.'

'Oh, all right, be like that.'

He sighed and went on eating grapes, two and three at a time. Kate looked at the clock. It was only twenty to four. He could only have been here a minute or two but it seemed like ages. If Sophie came now and looked through the glass doors and saw him sitting on the bed, she might think she wasn't wanted and go away again . . .

She said, 'It really was most awfully nice of you to come, Robin,' but he didn't take the hint. Just looked at her vaguely, as if his mind was far away. She felt so impatient that she wanted to scream, thump the bed-clothes . . .

At last he said, 'I came to tell you something. I've seen Squib.'

She sat bolt upright, so suddenly that it hurt her stomach. She said, '*Ow!*' and rocked backwards and forwards.

'Don't bust your stitches, girl!' He grinned; now he had begun, it was easy to go on. 'In Turner's Tower, at a window, quite high up. Just his face looking out and just for a minute, but it was him all right!'

She was breathing very deeply. 'Did you – did you *speak* to him?'

'No chance to. The Tower's where the housekeeper lives. Or perhaps she's just the cook, I'm not sure. Anyway, she came down for her paper and I asked her and she said he wasn't there. So there's something pretty odd going on and I've got an idea...'

He stopped because she didn't seem to be listening. Her eyes were wide and fixed in a stare. She seemed to be staring right through him.

She said, 'He's not a ghost, I knew he wasn't!' She laughed and the colour came and went in her face; she reached out to the bedside locker and took a sheet of paper from the drawer. 'Look at that!'

He pulled a face. 'Lucky I'm not vain, isn't it?'

'Not the drawing of you, stupid ape. T'other one. *Him.*'

The paper was crumpled. He smoothed it out on his knee. He said, 'She's got that funny look of his just right. Dead clever, your Mum.'

She said, 'I've been lying here, thinking. At first I thought, if he was a ghost, then my mother couldn't have seen him. Not clearly enough to draw him. I mean, being grown-up. But then I thought, perhaps she might have after all since it's her *son*. Do you see?'

'Oh, it's clear as mud,' Robin said, and then went on quickly, afraid he might have hurt her, ''Course I see, but it's beside the point, really. I don't say people don't see ghosts sometimes but he's not one. He couldn't be, too many of us saw him. *I* saw him and I don't see ghosts, I'm just not that psychic sort of person.'

'I know. I think I only thought he might be because the other thing seemed too good to be true.'

She was smiling. He felt cold, watching her smile like that. He said, 'What other thing' – and held his breath.

'Well.' Her smile deepened, dimpling the corners of her mouth. 'That he's Rupert come back!'

He let out his breath in a long sigh. He sought for something to say and it came to him. 'He can't be, can he? I mean, your mother would have recognized him.'

'He's older. And she's quite sure he's dead. You know what it's like, you see people when you're not expecting to, you don't always recognize them.'

He thought, that's cunning! Then, *Mad people are cunning!* He said desperately, 'You don't believe that, you can't! I mean, how could it be him?'

Her smile went. 'I don't know, do I? I haven't worked it out yet.'

'Have you told anyone? Have you told your *mother*?' Poor Mrs Pollack, that would be cruel! He said, 'You mustn't tell her!'

Her eyes were big and scornful. She said, 'Of course I shan't till I'm sure! Do you think I'm daft, Robin Tite?' – sounding so sane, if a bit cross, that he felt lightened sudddenly as if a weight had gone from his back. Then she looked at the clock at the end of the ward and said, in a quite different voice, 'Oh, it's four o'clock already!'

He said, 'I'm sorry I was late.'

'I didn't mean that. I meant Sophie. Sophie was coming.'

'Sophie? But she couldn't. She's gone.'

He had spoken without thinking; as soon as he saw the look on her face he wished he'd been struck dumb.

He stammered, 'They've m-moved away. D-didn't she t-tell you?'

She stared at him, biting her lip. Then she went red, so red that he felt the heat rise up in his own face. He tried to think of something to say but there seemed to be nothing. The bell went for the end of visiting time and there was still nothing, so he just said, 'Well, good-bye then,' and walked away up the long ward.

Kate watched him go. His trousers were shiny at the back and his school blazer was too short in the sleeves. When he had gone through the doors, she lay on her side and closed her eyes. She thought, *If only I hadn't been sick, she'd have told me*, and then heard her mother's voice, in her head. *Oh Kate, if only you hadn't gone in the sea without telling me . . .*

She pulled the blankets over her head and tried counting to stop herself crying. It didn't work: she could feel her face creasing up and the water coming into her mouth. She doubled her fists and pressed them into her cheeks and tried to think of a poem, and then, when that didn't work either, thought of Rupert instead; drifting happily out to sea, not scared at all but safe in his rubber ring until a fisherman picked him up and took him home and brought him up as his own little boy.

Or perhaps he'd been washed up on some foreign shore . . .

Kidnapped, Robin thought, lying awake in the hot night, *kidnapped and held to ransom* . . .

Not a ghost, not a dead boy come back to life, but some rich man's son. Kidnapped some time ago, long enough to grow out of his clothes. They hadn't dared buy him new, for fear of attracting attention.

It fitted all right, the babyish gear, the 'Auntie'. Not his Auntie, of course, but his *keeper*: the gang that had stolen him had paid her to hide him. A good hiding place too – who would look for a missing child in an Old People's Home? They'd smuggled him in one dark night and she'd kept him, locked up in the Tower. He was so scared, or just so little, perhaps, that when he found some way to escape he didn't run away, only to the park, to play with Sammy and Prue.

He thought, *What gang?* The Wild Ones? They were only boys, like the gardener's boy at the Tower. They might seem frightening, roaring round with noisy bikes and flick-knives, but it was all swagger and bluff. Kidnappers were real criminals, and dangerous. Cold hearts, cool minds . . .

Robin felt his throat constrict. But alarm always swelled in the dark. It was all right, really. He was safe in his bed for the moment; Squib was safe in the Tower. Plenty of time to think, to work out the best thing to do . . .

He tossed and turned, searching for a cool place in the sheets. It was so hot and still, the air stuffy, even with the window wide open. Stuffy, and smelling of bonfires . . .

'Fireworks,' Prue said from the doorway. 'Robin, can you smell fireworks?'

Robin sat up. Prue's nightgown flickered white in the darkness. She padded across the room, bare feet squeaking on lino, and stood by the window. 'Oh Robin,' she said in a delighted voice, 'Come and *look*.'

He scolded her, 'What are you doing, don't you know it's the middle of the night?' but he got out of bed and joined her. On the other side of the road the trees of Turner's Tower were black against a rosy glow; as they watched, a shower of sparks flew upwards, then cascaded down.

'It *is* fireworks,' Prue said, and clapped her hands together. 'Oh, how *lovely*.'

For a moment, Robin almost believed her. It looked so pretty and harmless; the pink, sunset sky and the yellow sparks, like golden rain. Then he said, 'Prue, you daft ha'porth. It's a fire. A real fire!'

Even then he wasn't afraid; things take time to sink in and though he was old for his age, and responsible, he was still only a boy. He began to pull clothes on over his pyjamas, fingers turned into thumbs with excitement.

'If you're going to look,' Prue said, 'then I'm coming too.'

He hopped on one foot while he tied the shoe on the other. 'Oh no you're not, Miss!'

'Yes I am!'

'*No*. Mum 'ud be mad.'

Mad at him too, if she found out he'd gone, but never mind that. He could get round her; Prue couldn't. He said, 'It's all right for me. I'm a boy, and I'm older.'

'Pig,' she said. 'Grammar school yob.'

'Where'd you pick up that charming expression?'

'Never you mind.'

There was enough light to see her mouth turning down. If she started to bawl, Mum would wake up. He said, 'Be a good girl and watch from the window and I'll buy you a present tomorrow. Mint chocs, a whole packet.'

'Packet of cigarettes,' she said.

'*What?*' He was shocked and sounded it; Prue giggled nervously.

'Not for me, for my friend.'

'What friend you got, smokes cigarettes?'

'No one you know.'

'If I get them, will you shut up and stay here?'

'Packet of *twenty*?'

'Oh, all right!'

Prue smiled, the rare, wide, curving smile that lifted her face and made her beautiful. *Oh, when she gets her own way!* Robin thought as he went down the stairs, and then, *But she wanted to come to the fire . . .*

That puzzled him – she must be dead keen on this mysterious friend if she didn't mind staying behind – but there was no time to think about it now. No time to *think* – as he ran up the road the fire engine swept past, clanging bell and glittering brass, and turned into the Old People's Home. Robin ran after it, caught up in excitement, along the winding, wooded drive and round the side of the house. The old people were out on the lawn with overcoats over their nightclothes, but the main building was safe for the moment. It was the Tower that was burning, a furnace roaring up inside its black skeleton . . .

For a moment, Robin felt only amazement. This was a splendid thing to see: the Tower burning like a torch in the night. As he watched, one window seemed to melt in the heat – one second it was there, the next it had quite disappeared – and a yellow tongue shot out and licked upwards. There was a rattling, whispering sound as the ivy blackened and began to burn, the leaves curling up crisply like rashers of bacon. And then a tearing, splintering crash from the inside of the Tower, as if a floor or a staircase had fallen.

Robin felt his heart squeezed tight in his chest. It was as if he had been picked up and held by some enormous hand and then dropped from a height. Back on solid ground, he gasped and looked round, but apart from the helmeted firemen the only people in sight were from the big house, the staff of the Home and their charges, huddling together on the grass. No child anywhere. No small, pale figure . . .

The firemen were playing the hose on the side of the Tower nearest the house; a thick, foaming snake of water that seemed to have a strong, curving life of its own. Two of them manned the hydrant; Robin ran to them and clutched at a uniformed arm. His teeth were chattering as if they had come loose from his gums; it was like trying to speak through a mouthful of stones, but he managed it. 'Did they get the people out?'

The man shook his arm free and snapped, 'Get back with the others.' Then he glanced down at Robin and added, more kindly, 'It's all right, son, there's no one in there.'

No one alive, at any rate. The Tower was a contained funnel of fire, an incinerator, white-hot in the centre. Robin stood still; frozen and staring.

The firemen said, 'Clear off now, do as you're told,' and he went on dragging feet, dreadful thoughts whirling through his mind. Had she left him there, left him behind to die? She could have done; no one would know except his kidnappers and they wouldn't give her away. If his parents hadn't paid up the ransom money they might even be glad to be rid of him . . .

Robin couldn't believe this, it was too terrible, but just thinking about it made him shiver. He thought, *He must have got out, he must* – and ran to the group on the lawn, pushing among them, looking desperately into their faces. Shrunken cheeks, softly pursed mouths; old eyes looking back at him, blank with bewilderment or terror. Someone small in a wheel-chair – he caught his breath, but it was only an old, old lady, tucked up under blankets. She was looking at him. He said, 'There's a boy, have you seen a boy?' and she smiled suddenly and happily as if he had said something funny, her little face wrinkling up like a prune. She said, in a bright, chirrupy voice, 'You know, we might have been burned in our beds. Burned alive!'

70

Robin began to cry. He stumbled away from the old people, tears blinding his eyes. Someone caught his shoulder; gripped hard enough to hurt. 'Steady on now,' Colonel Wittering said.

He was fully dressed: silk cravat at his neck, pearl-topped stick in his hand. He smiled, showing yellow fangs. 'Nothing to blubber about. No danger. Not enough wind to set fire to the house.'

Robin said, 'There's a b-boy in the Tower. Or there was. Have you seen him?'

'Boy?' The Colonel spoke as if this were some strange kind of animal. He looked closely at Robin. 'No boy, far as I know. Only Starvation Sal, and she's gone.'

Robin stared at him. Tears dried on his cheeks; he could feel the skin tightening.

'The cook,' Colonel Wittering said. 'Or so-called. Lumpy potatoes, fried eggs like plastic jokes, cigarette ash in the soup. She went a couple of days ago – largely my doing, I'm proud to say. I'd organized a small mutiny.'

Robin swallowed. 'She had a boy. A little boy. She kept him in the Tower.'

The Colonel's eyebrows rose. 'Did she, by Jove. I wouldn't have thought her that human! Suppose she took him off with her then, though I can't say I saw him. Saw *her* go, though! Saw her off the premises lock, stock and barrel.' He smiled at Robin and rubbed the side of his nose with his forefinger. 'Budgerigar and laundry basket, rather!'

'*Laundry basket?*'

'Pinched, shouldn't wonder. Great big thing – hotel and hospital size. Went off in the back of a van, sitting on top of it. Bird cage on her lap.'

Robin thought, *Sam's wicked witch!* He could have laughed with relief. Then he thought, *That's not so funny!* Squib was alive; he'd left in the basket. But how would he find him now?

He said, 'Where'd she go, do you know?'

71

The Colonel shook his head. 'She'd hardly leave me her card, would she? Nor Matron, neither. They'd had high words, I understand. Matron was missing some spoons, but the woman denied it.'

Robin said, 'What's her name?'

'Starvation Sal. Famine Flossie. Not just bad food you know, but mean with it. Lining her own purse, shouldn't wonder.'

No address. A boy called Squib. A woman called Starvation Sal . . .

Robin said, 'She must have had a real name, though.'

But the Colonel was watching the fire which was under control now: a glow inside the black, gutted Tower and a sharp smell of ash.

Robin touched his hand. 'You must have called her something. I mean, to her *face*.'

The Colonel looked down at him with a slightly puzzled expression. 'Just, *my good woman*, what else should I call her?' he said.

12

WHEN Prue got to the shed, Sammy was already there, squatting on the ground beside the Wild One and rubbing two pebbles together. There was a look of solemn concentration on his face.

'Try now,' the boy said, and Sammy sniffed the pebbles and laughed and nodded.

'Told you, didn't I? Smells of sparks, don't it?'

'Gunpowder,' Sammy said, eyes wide and shining. 'Smells of gunpowder.'

'He doesn't know what gunpowder smells like,' Prue said, speaking in her most grown-up voice, but the Wild One didn't even look at her. He was watching Sammy.

'If you go on, you c'n make the sparks fly,' he said.

Prue stood there, breathing painfully – Turner's Wood still scared her when she was alone and she had run fast and got a stitch in her side – and feeling jealous. It was always like this: him talking to Sammy and showing him things and leaving her out.

She said, 'I brought you a present,' and he did look at her then; just one quick glance at her face, then down to the cigarettes in her hand.

'D'you nick 'em?'

She shook her head. 'I got them from my brother. I mean, he gave me the money. He owed it me.' She tossed the packet on to his lap and went on, very quickly in case he should feel he had to thank her, 'Did you see the fire?'

He peered at her shyly through his thicket of hair. 'Wasn't here, was I? I was down home with me Dad.'

'Where do you live?' Sammy said, sitting back on his heels and staring.

The boy looked suspicious as he often did when he was asked a direct question. As if he felt threatened by something. But he said, 'The caravan site. Down by the gravel pit. Not for much longer, though.'

'I'd love to live in a caravan,' Sammy said. 'I'd stop a different place every night, an' catch rabbits like a gipsy, an' light fires, an' never, ever, go to school.'

'S'not that sort of caravan, just a lousy old bus without wheels.' But the boy smiled. Sammy could always make him smile, Prue thought.

She said, 'What d'you mean, not for much longer? You're not going away!'

He shrugged his shoulders and yawned, rather elaborately. 'Jus' clearing out. It was all right, jus' me and me Dad, but the old bitch is back and I can't stick her.'

'That's a rude word,' Sammy said, frowning severely, and the boy grinned at him.

'Old witch, then. Much the same thing. Your old witch from the Tower.'

Prue's voice went up high and squeaky with horror. 'Is she your *mother*?' She had never seen the woman in the Tower and had a muddled picture in her mind: partly the old lady she and Sammy had spoken to, and partly a real witch with a tall hat and a broomstick and one long, pointed tooth.

The boy said shortly, 'Step. Me Mum's dead.'

Prue thought of her mother dying. It was something that often frightened her in the middle of the night, especially if she had gone to bed angry. Her mother dying and her father marrying again, some wicked stepmother who would beat her and lock her up in the dark cupboard under the stairs . . .

She said hoarsely, 'Is she wicked to you?'

He frowned, lit a cigarette from the packet she had brought him, and drew on it till the tip glowed bright. He said, through

74

a cloud of smoke, 'Me? Oh, she don't bother *me*. It's Dad she goes for, nag, nag, nag, till he bashes her up. Then we all have to look out. My Dad's O.K. if you leave him alone but he's a shocker when he's roused. She went for the police last time but they were scared to come in. Just stood outside listening to him cursing and blinding and told her to clear off with the boy till he'd simmered down.'

The children listened, round-eyed. This was a story to Sammy, like Hansel and Gretel. But Prue felt the difference and it made her uncomfortable. She said, 'I didn't know you had a brother.'

'No more I have. He ain't me Dad's, nor hers neither. She jus' got landed with him and it's him makes the trouble. He's not a bad kid but he whines and that starts her off nagging and then Dad gets his rag out. I clear off quick but she never learns, just goes on wagging her tongue till he lams into her. That shuts her up for a bit when she's stopped yelling blue murder.'

'Why doesn't she put a spell on him?' Sammy said.

The boy blinked at him. Then he laughed and stubbed out his cigarette. 'Oh, she ain't that sort of witch. Jus' the kind eats little boys.' He rolled his eyes and smacked his lips and said, 'Bones an' all,' in a growly, menacing voice that made Sammy giggle. Then he winked at Prue.

She said proudly, "Course *I* don't believe that. Only Sam. He's a *baby*.'

'I aren't,' Sammy said. 'I know people don't eat bones. They stick in your throat.'

'Well, maybe she just stews 'em up.' The boy winked at Prue again, and her heart swelled with love. He said, 'That's what we get to eat most nights! Human stew! Smell it cooking soon as you get near the site!'

Sammy shivered with pleasure, tucking his hands between his thighs and rocking backwards and forwards on the ground. 'Can I come and see? Can I come and see your caravan?'

'No. Not 'less you want to end up in the pot!' He pulled a

mock fierce face, then sighed, and got to his feet. He took a spade from the shed and slung it in the barrow.

'Oh *please*.' Prue jumped up and down with excitement. 'We could come when she's out.'

'I'm not scared of *her*,' Sammy said. 'I never seen inside a caravan.'

The boy looked at them both. 'I said no, didn't I? What d'you think I'm doing, running a nursery school? Bad enough having you hanging round here all the time without going on outings.'

Prue felt sick. She whispered, 'We only asked,' and gazed at the ground. A big, plum-coloured ant was running along, pulling a leaf four times its own size. Prue stared at it hard as if she had never seen an ant before. Her eyes began to burn.

The boy said, a bit uneasily, 'They're a rough lot, down the site. Your Mum wouldn't like it. I bet she don't know you come here, even. Talking to me, an' that. Him *smoking*. I'm the one 'ud catch it, not you.' He waited a minute but she wouldn't answer, or even look at him, just stood as if she'd been struck dumb; a dumb statue with turned-down eyes, turned-down mouth. In the end he said, 'Well. Ta for the cigs,' and went off along the path, pushing the barrow and whistling.

Sammy said, 'Prue.'

She was squatting on her haunches, still watching the ant and trying to help it carry the leaf by lifting one end with a twig. When Sam spoke, she looked up briefly and blinked and said, 'What?' in a surprised and distant voice as if she had been locked away with her thoughts for such a long time that she had quite forgotten he was there.

Sammy squatted beside her. He said, 'Don't hurt the ant.'

'I'm not. I'm watching it. For Nature Study.'

He said, 'It's like a lorry, the long, double kind. The way it bends in the middle. Come *on*, Prue.'

'Where?' She sounded bored and cross.

'You know. Down to the caravan.' He put his warm, small

76

hand on her knee. 'We don't have to go with *him*. We can go by ourselves.'

She threw the twig away and stood up, scuffing earth over the ant's track with her foot. 'We're not allowed down the pit.'

'T'isn't the pit. It's the site. Mum never said about the site.'

'Same thing, though. The site's near the pit.'

'She won't know.' He tugged her sleeve and she looked at him and saw his eyes were shining bright as if water had been poured over them. 'We might see the old witch,' he said.

Prue felt so empty and miserable she didn't care what she did. *Hanging round all the time* – the awful words rang in her head as she followed Sammy through the wood. He didn't like her. He hated her. She hated herself. She wished she was dead.

Perhaps she would die, then he'd be sorry. Get pneumonia and die slowly; or quickly, crossing the road. The thought cheered her up as they passed the park and came to the end of the footpath and she took Sammy's hand and swung it, to show she felt better. They went through the main street and out of the town; across the humped bridge over the river and down to the waste land, past the weir. This was forbidden territory: the rutted, dirt road leading to the gravel pit with its deep, velvety water and tall machinery that made a shug-shugging sound as wheels turned and ballast rattled. The caravan site lay between the pit and the river, marked off by a paling fence that was broken in so many places that only cars used the proper entrance: people took the most convenient route.

'There's no old buses here,' Sammy said.

'This is the posh end. They've got gardens, even.' Prue shaded her eyes to look into the slanting sun. 'I expect the bus is down nearer the pit. It's noisier there and not so nice.'

They walked along the dirt road until it petered out and the pit widened, almost joining the river. Only a narrow ridge of land edged with bulrushes led to the fields beyond; the ground was marshy under their feet and the wind blew off the water bringing a sweet, rotting, dustbin smell.

A hooter wailed and the machinery stopped clanking. At first it seemed blissfully quiet and then other sounds crowded in; birds calling, the suck of water in the reeds, the sharp *clap* of a swan's wings. 'There's a nest,' Sammy said, pressing close to Prue as the bird snaked its neck and hissed. 'She won't hurt if we don't go too near,' Prue said. 'D'you think that's the bus?'

It was right at the end of the site, very close to the pit; an old, single-decker, set on concrete piles, with most of its windows boarded up. So run-down and desolate that the oldest and shabbiest caravans looked like palaces beside it. 'There's no one there,' Sammy said.

'Yes there is.' Prue pointed. 'There's washing out.'

Between two poles, a line of clothes billowed in the breeze: vests and underpants, a woman's cotton dress.

'D'you think *she's* inside?' Sammy said.

Prue felt him shiver but it only excited her. Nothing could happen to them, not in broad daylight with other people in easy reach, sitting on the steps of their caravans in the evening sun. And besides, in spite of the washing, the bus looked safely untenanted: no smoke from the chimney, no sign of life . . .

'No cooking tonight,' Prue said, and giggled, shrilly. 'No human stew.'

'Sssh . . .' Sammy was pale as a peeled nut. 'Oh Prue, let's go home.'

'Not till we've *looked*. Come on, scaredy-cat.' She took his hand and dragged him forward. At the front of the bus, steps led up to a closed door and the windows had glass in them but were too high to see into. 'You'll have to get on my back,' Prue said. And then, when Sammy shut his eyes and shook his head, 'Well I can't stand on yours, I'm too heavy, aren't I?'

Sammy opened his eyes and sighed. Prue bent over and heaved him up, pick-a-back. He scrabbled with his hands on the rusty sides of the bus and peered in through dirty glass.

At first he could see nothing, it was so murky dark. Then, as his eyes got used to it, he made out a table with newspaper spread on it and the remains of a meal: mugs, plates, an old cornflake packet. Beyond the table, bunks against the side of the bus, and on the bottom bunk, a boy sitting. Not doing anything, just sitting with his thin legs dangling, and staring at the window.

Sammy said, 'Oh, it's Squib!'

Prue gasped and staggered and he fell off her back. 'It's Squib,' he repeated. They looked at each other and then up at the window. Minutes seemed to pass and then the little boy's face appeared, looking down. His hands pressed flat against the window, like starfish. His mouth moved. 'He's saying *Sammy*,' Sam said, and laughed out loud.

Prue ran up the steps to the door of the bus. She pushed and pushed, but it didn't move. 'Locked,' she said under her breath, and thought, *Prison* . . . She looked round but no one was watching; all the people that had been sitting on their caravan steps had gone inside or vanished somewhere. No one around suddenly; no sound, except for the wind in the reeds and the gulls, dipping and crying over the ruffled water of the pit.

Nothing to be afraid of, but Prue was afraid.

Sammy said, from the bottom of the steps, 'He remembers me. He said *Sammy*. He wants to come out and play.'

'He can't,' Prue said. 'He's locked in.'

'Bash the door down then!' Sammy looked at her confidently: Prue was so old, so strong, she could do anything! He said, 'It's all right, Prue. The old witch isn't there.'

'I know.' Prue tried to smile but her face had gone stiff. What she was afraid of she didn't know, only that it was something more frightening than a hundred old witches.

She said, in a choking voice, 'Oh Sammy, come home . . .'

13

'SOMEONE must know her name,' Kate said. 'Matron must. Even if she doesn't know her address.'

'I suppose so,' Robin said. He felt too lazy to talk, lying on his back in Kate's garden with a good tea inside him and the grass smelling of summer. Too lazy, even, to brush off the little brown husks that floated down from the beech trees and tickled his face . . .

'What do you mean, *you suppose so*?'

He sighed and sat up. 'All right then, *yes*. I mean, I know someone must. D'you think I didn't think? But then I thought, what's the use? It might just be something like Smith, or Brown, or Jones, and even if it wasn't, what good would it do knowing? Just her name? I shouldn't think she's the sort would be in *Who's Who*, exactly. Not even the telephone book, that fly-by-night sort of person. And then again, I thought, well, I could *ask*. Wouldn't hurt. But I was embarrassed a bit. I mean, it looked *nosey*.'

'Do you mind what things look like?'

'Well, yes. A bit. More than you do anyway. The thing is, if I was really sure something was wrong it wouldn't matter, but I can't be, can I?' He picked a beech husk off his sleeve and examined it closely. 'What I mean is, you think something in the middle of the night but come morning it's different. I mean, he could have been kidnapped, of course, and it was exciting thinking that, but then I thought, it's not really likely.'

'Why not? She was hiding him, wasn't she?'

'Or just keeping him dark. She was the cook in the Old People's Home, maybe she wasn't supposed to have her son with her, living in.'

Kate said, 'Things don't have to be dull to be true.'

She lay in a long, wicker chair, her head on a cushion, and stared up at the sky. Her eyes closed and Robin thought she was dozing, but after a little she went on, speaking softly and dreamily. 'Suppose it wasn't a fisherman rescued him, but a rich man with a yacht. A rich man with no children. Perhaps he'd had some and they'd died and his wife was dead too, or couldn't have any more. He'd want someone to leave his fortune to, wouldn't he? Someone who'd be a comfort in his lonely old age. He picks this boy out of the sea and it's like a miracle, a dream answered. Just a little boy, old enough to talk and tell him his name, but that's all. We hadn't been here long, he wouldn't know his address and the rich man wouldn't try to find out, or not very hard, anyway. Because he wanted to keep him and bring him up as his own . . .'

Robin shifted restlessly on the grass. This was the first time she'd talked like this since that day in hospital. He said, with a forced grin, 'I thought you'd given that up. All that silly nonsense!'

She turned her head on the pillow. 'No sillier than your story, is it? His being kidnapped! In fact it fits in! If this man was very rich or had enemies who wanted to get their own back!'

'So they kidnapped the boy and brought him here, next door to his mother and sister? The arm of coincidence isn't that long.' Robin went on grinning at her but he felt terrible inside. She seemed so calm, so *happy*. Could you be happy and mad? She didn't look mad, just pale as a lily and thinner than she used to be. He said, 'Well, truth is stranger than fiction.'

She looked at him carefully as if trying to make out if he was humouring her, and frowned a little. 'Of course I don't know that's what's happened, it's just something I worked out because it fits what I feel . . .' She hesitated, her eyes searching his face, and then blushed like a rose. 'What I feel in my *heart*,' she said, clenching her fist and thudding it down on her

81

chest, 'that he's in some kind of awful *danger*. You do believe that, don't you?'

He wished he didn't have to answer. And not just because he didn't know. He didn't *want* to believe it, he realized suddenly. Because if he did, he would have to do something about it, tell someone, and he shrank from that. He would feel such a fool.

She said, 'Well, do you?' and he sighed heavily and stared at the grass and selected a long, juicy blade and chewed on it thoughtfully, acting the part of a person who wasn't accustomed to giving his valuable opinions lightly. But though he wasn't looking at her, he knew she was not in the least taken in. She was watching him steadily and waiting . . .

Then the garden door crashed open and he looked up and saw Prue and Sammy. He thought, *saved by the bell*, and jumped up, discomfort and indecision swept away on a wave of comfortable anger. What did they think they were doing, bursting into Kate's garden without being asked? Kate didn't want to be bothered with kids, only three days out of hospital, and they hadn't even shut the gate! He opened his mouth to give them a piece of his mind – and then looked at Prue.

She was stumping along with her cold rice pudding look. He said, 'What's up with you?' and she stared at him for a minute, sullen and scowling. Then her face seemed to crack like a dropped plate and she flung herself at him, bulleting into his stomach, wrapping legs and arms round him.

She began to cry in a painful, heaving, gasping way. He held her tight and spoke in a soft, monotonous voice, to soothe her. 'All right girl, it's all right, ssh, Prue, there . . .'

Kate said anxiously, 'What's the matter, is she hurt?' and he shook his head. It was just one of Prue's turns and it was wearing itself out now; her sobs quietening.

'What's it all about?' he said, holding her away from him and looking down into her face, but it was too soon to ask; she twisted out of his arms and turned her back and shut her eyes and stuck her fingers in her ears. Deaf, dumb and blind . . .

Robin wanted to laugh but stopped himself. He said gravely to Sammy, 'You tell me, then.'

Sammy's mouth was twitching and his eyes shining as if he knew a delightful secret. But he wasn't prepared to tell it, not straightaway. He put his hands in his pockets and wriggled inside his trousers. 'I dunno, do I?' he said. 'She's been like this all the way.'

'All the way where?'

'From the pit.' Sammy's eyes were brilliant. 'We been down the gravel pit.'

'Oh,' Robin said. 'Oh, I see.' He looked at Kate. 'Guilt, that's it, then! She gets like this when she's done something she shouldn't. Though it's mostly when she wakes in the night.'

'Poor Prue. It's all right, we won't tell.' Kate got up from her chair and touched the little girl's shoulder to comfort her, but Prue shrugged her hand away.

Robin said, 'It's not that, just that she feels bad. She gets a terrible conscience.'

'She's just scared,' Sammy said scornfully. 'She's just scared of the silly old witch.'

Robin and Kate looked at each other. Both began smiling.

Sammy's eyes were round. 'She didn't want to come and look for her, even, but I made her. *I* wasn't scared but she was. She made me look in the bus.'

'Did you see her?' Robin was grinning broadly now. 'What did she look like?'

'Long, straggly hair?' Kate said. 'And grey, slitty eyes, and a sort of thin, crooked face, all bones and hollows?'

Sammy giggled. 'Oh, she wasn't there. Only Squib. I thought she'd eaten him up, but she hadn't. I expect he's not fat enough yet.'

Robin and Kate stared at him. The warm summer air

seemed to turn cold and blow through them. Their mouths hung open.

It was Prue broke the silence. She opened her eyes, took her fingers out of her ears, and swung round to face them. 'Oh Robin, it's *awful*,' she said. 'He's a *prisoner*. You got to do something quick!'

14

'No point in just bursting down there, we ought to *plan*,' Robin said. And to Kate, 'You're not fit to go out yet, your mother won't like it.' And to Sammy, 'D'you know what the time is? Your bedtime, nearly.'

No use, of course. Three against one. He could stop Sammy and Prue perhaps, but not Kate. Her legs were wobbly from being in bed and her scar hurt when she stood upright but wild horses wouldn't hold her. Her skin had a pearly look as if a light shone behind it and her eyes glowed with visions. She listened to his arguments and then spat one word. 'Pro-crastinator.'

'What's that?' Sammy asked, liking the sound of this.

'Putting off till tomorrow what you could do today.' She tossed her head at Robin. 'You could make a career of it, why don't you? Set up a shop to sell excuses for not doing things.'

'It's an idea,' Robin said. 'The Look-Before-You-Leap shop.'

But he couldn't let them go alone. Didn't want to, when it came down to it. Talk came more naturally to him than action, but he could act when he had to. A bit slow off the mark, perhaps, had to be prodded over the first fence, but gathered speed after. *Overtake them all at the end*, he thought, writing a sort of school report on himself in his head as he followed them down the path. And then, *What do they think they're going to do when they get there?*

Not that he knew, either. It was that had held him back really: he liked to see his way plain. If Prue was right and Squib was a prisoner, then the odds were he'd been right all along: it was a kidnapping, a police matter. Should he go to the police? That might be dangerous. They might kill Squib if they knew the police were after them: kidnappers often did that. He'd have to do something first to prevent it, but what could he do, with only a sick girl and two little kids to help him? He thought, wait and see, you'll think of something and added a sentence to his report. *Robin is a resourceful boy.*

His spirits rose and he quickened his pace, catching the others up as they crossed the river and came to the waste land and the dirt road. Ahead of them the pit machinery reared up like the skeletons of ancient creatures, gaunt and naked against a rose and yellow sky.

'Prehistoric,' he said to Kate.

'What?'

'Those cranes. Dinosaurs. Tyrannosorus Rex.'

'Oh *you* ...' But she was smiling. 'They're beautiful,' she said.

He pulled a face. 'Not a word I'd use. The sunset is though.'

It was a lovely evening, warm and golden. The caravan site was alive; children playing, men standing in groups, talking and smoking. As they approached the far end of the site there were fewer people about but the air still bubbled with voices and laughter. Robin thought, *Nothing really bad can be happening here ...*

'There's the bus,' Prue said, and stopped short. The others walked on, then looked back. She was rooted still, and staring.

'Afraid of the old witch?' Robin said.

She shook her head. Her lips were trembling. 'She's locked him up. In the dark. Like a cupboard.'

'Not now,' Robin said. 'Look.'

The bus door was open. A thin column of smoke rose from the chimney.

Robin winked at Kate. 'Cannibal stew?'

She frowned at him. Then whispered, 'Do they really believe that?'

'Sammy does. Prue only half. And only that because

Sammy's so sure. If you really believe something, you can usually convince other people.'

'I haven't convinced you, have I? Not even half. You don't believe *me*.'

But she didn't seem to mind this. Her voice was light and cheerful, gently teasing him. She was looking so happy and confident, he thought he couldn't bear it. He said, 'I don't know. I really don't know.' He tried to laugh. 'Perhaps I'm just scared to!'

'*I'm* scared,' Prue said, coming up. She stood between them, clenched fist against her mouth. 'Oh Robin, make Sammy come back!'

He had gone through a hole in the paling fence and was trudging solidly up the slight incline towards the bus. As they watched, a woman came out and went to the washing line. Buttercup hair, crumpled cotton dress, bare legs white as cold mutton fat. 'That's her,' Robin said, 'The cook. His *jailer*.' His cheeks began to burn with excitement. Perhaps they could do something after all. If she was alone, no one else on guard. ... He thought. LOCAL BOY IN RESCUE DASH. A headline in a newspaper.

The woman stretched up to take down the clothes, her back to the bus. Squib appeared at the door, looking out. Kate said, 'Oh, he's there!' and Robin caught her arm. 'Wait,' he said. 'Don't rush things.'

Sammy began to run. A small figure, running and waving. The little boy watched him.

Robin said, 'Best leave it to Sammy. He'll get him to come out and play, she won't be suspicious of that. Get him away from the bus, that's the main thing.'

Squib came down the steps. Sammy had reached him now, was standing beside him. The fair head and the dark, close together. And the woman had turned and seen them ...

She waddled forward, draped in washing. Her voice came clear through the soft, still air. 'Get inside, you!' She dumped the clothes in a tin bath and stood, hands on hips. 'I told you to stay in and keep clean, didn't I? Can't turn my back for a minute! You'll do what you're told my lad, or I'll learn you.'

Squib crooked his arm in front of his face. She reached out and cuffed him; they heard the slap and saw his head jerk back. She said, 'Basket for you, that's what you're asking for, that's what you'll get,' and he began to wail thinly. Sammy began to back away and she shouted at him. 'You clear off or I'll clip you one too. Bloody kids hanging round, I won't have it.'

She went up the steps and inside, dragging Squib with her, leaving the door open. They heard him crying, not as Sammy or Prue would have cried if their mother had hit them, bawling with rage, but softly, despairingly, on one sad, whining note.

Robin and Kate stood, still and shocked. Sammy was running towards them, face screwed up. He ducked behind Kate like a frightened squirrel behind a tree trunk and then peered round, clutching her skirt and looking at Robin. Kate looked at him too. His heart went down to his boots. He said, 'I don't see what we can do.'

Kate said, 'Oh, Robin!'

He said, 'Well, you tell me,' but he walked slowly forward. No clear intention, just escaping from the look in her eyes. Through the gap in the fence and a few yards inside, feet heavy as lead. The whole site seemed to have fallen quiet suddenly, or perhaps that low, level weeping had driven out all other sounds. He looked round hopefully but only one person was near: a thin young woman standing at the door of her caravan, nursing a baby and looking towards the bus. He stopped near her, for comfort; she caught his eye and said, 'Poor kid, it's a sin and a shame.'

The tone of the crying changed; a gasping sob and then several shrill screams, like a train in a cutting. Robin felt as if he had swallowed a great draught of iced water: the chill ran right through him.

The screaming stopped. Somehow the silence was even more terrifying. Robin said, 'Someone ought to do something.'

The young woman heaved her baby up on her shoulder and patted its back. She smiled at Robin and he saw she had one tooth missing. She said, 'You'd need a nerve. Old Tarzan 'ud take you apart soon as look at you.'

'Tarzan?' Robin said, and as if to answer him, a man's voice came from the bus. No clear word, just a short, maddened bellow. He appeared at the door, a broad, stocky man, naked to the waist with a mat of dark hair on his chest and a heavy, bearded, scowling face. He slumped on the steps, yawning as if he had just woken up and rasping his face with a big hand like a spade. No sign of the woman but her nagging pursued him. 'Oh, it's all right for you, you can talk, talk costs nothing, suit you to get him out from under your feet, I dare say, but I've got enough to do, day in, day out, without extra. Let him out, where'd it stop – in and out, back and fore, messing and humbugging about, getting himself filthy, picking up habits, bringing in muck on his feet, who'd clean it up, tell me that? Not you, catch you doing a hand's turn, bar making a rod for my back . . .'

The man shouted, 'Shut your trap,' but he didn't move – too lazy or too sleepy, perhaps – and her voice went relentlessly on.

The young woman wiped the baby's mouth and sighed. 'We're in for a fine night of it, see that with half an eye. He'll finish her off one of these days and I can't say I blame him.' She had a plain, pale, bony face; sharp and wary, but kind. She looked at Robin and said, 'I'd clear off if I were you, he don't like people watching.'

She went into her caravan and shut the door, quite loudly. The man got to his feet, glancing in the direction of the sound as he did so, and his eye fell on Robin who stood still, not daring to move, feeling horribly exposed and helpless. But the man only stared at him for a minute, yawning and scratching his stomach. Then he turned and lumbered into the bus.

Robin flew back to the others as if a spring had snapped and released him. They stood where he'd left them, on the dirt road near the water, the little ones clinging to Kate. They were too scared even to cry, but she was angry, not frightened. She said, 'Oh, those terrible people! We've got to get him out of there.'

Robin nodded. He had no doubts about that. Only he had to think how. He said, 'It's Saturday, isn't it? He's not the sort 'ud stay home, Saturday night. Once he's had his tea, he'll be off to the pub, then we'll see what to do. Get *her* out of the bus somehow, bang on the window or make a noise round the back. One of us act as decoy while the others creep into the bus.'

Sammy said, 'The old witch won't go. She'll stay and she'll eat him.'

Terror had blanched his face and made his eyes shine like dark pools. Robin squatted down, level with him. 'She's not a witch, Sammy.'

'She *is*. You don't know.' He thrust out his lip. 'I want to go *home*.'

Robin looked at Kate. She said softly, 'We've got to have Sammy. He won't come for us. And Prue's too frightened, I think.'

He took Sammy's hand. He said, 'Listen, Sam. There aren't any witches, only in books. She's not a witch, she's his keeper. They've kidnapped Squib you see, her and that man, and we've got to rescue him. I'm not sure how yet, I've got to work it out, but you can help if you're sensible and do what you're told, and we'll get him away and take him back to his Mummy and Daddy.'

'Not his Daddy,' Kate murmured. Then she gave a nervous little laugh and cleared her throat as if she wished she hadn't spoken. Robin looked up and saw she had gone scarlet. *She's scared*, he thought, *she's scared it's not true now it's come to the point*, and he felt sorry for her but glad too, because it meant she wasn't mad, she knew it couldn't really be Rupert locked up in that bus; it was just a sort of daydream she'd had, a tale she'd been telling herself . . .

''Tisn't true,' Prue said suddenly. ''Tisn't true, none of it, not kidnappers nor witches, it's just a lot of rotten old *lies*.'

Her face distorted and she began to cry. Robin tried to take hold of her to calm her, but she flailed her arms and butted him with her head like a little goat. 'Let her go,' Kate said, distracting his attention for a second, and Prue tore herself out of his grasp and ran away, back down the road. 'Didn't want her screaming and attracting attention,' Kate said, looking apprehensively towards the bus.

A light showed yellow through the windows, but there was no other sign of life. Nor in the rest of the site, they slowly realized, looking round in the gathering twilight: lamps were lit but doors were closed. A few stray dogs sniffed round dust-bins, but the only human being they could see was Prue, and she was almost out of sight now, her cotton dress fluttery and pale, like a moth in the dusk.

Sammy said, 'She's scared. She gets awful scared. She's a silly juggins, isn't she, Robin?'

'I'm not so sure.' Robin looked at the deepening sky, the black water of the pit. 'Gets dark quickly,' he said. 'Doesn't it?'

Sammy said importantly, 'I'm not scared of the dark, only of witches.'

'If that's all, then you're lucky,' Kate said. 'Listen – I think she's started again.'

'Nag, nag, nag,' Sammy said. 'That's what the Wild One says.'

They looked at him, puzzled, but this was no time to ask questions: the man was shouting in the bus. His voice rose above the woman's in a series of sharp, angry bursts, like cannon fire. She screeched back at him; he was silenced for a minute and then started up again, loud and furious. Calling her dreadful names . . .

The children listened, fascinated. Sammy said, 'Oh, the *words.*'

'Don't listen,' Robin said. 'It's not suitable.'

'I can't help it. I'm not *deaf*. Did you hear what he *said* . . .'

'Shut up,' Robin said sharply.

Kate giggled suddenly, her hand held to her side as if she had a pain.

Robin was shocked, but only briefly. It was awful, of course, embarrassing and awful, but it was funny too. His mouth began to twitch.

Sammy stared at them both. 'What are you laughing at?' he said. 'It's not funny. My friend Squib's in there.'

15

PRUE sobbed as she ran. Eyes screwed up, hair flying, legs moving like pistons. Running as if something dark and terrible and unknown ran behind her, but no coherent thought in her head, except that she wanted her mother. She said, 'Mum, Mum, oh *Mum*,' seeing nothing but the uneven ground that seemed to race backwards under her feet, hearing nothing but her own gasping breath. She didn't even see the Wild One, pushing his broken-down bike off the road and on to the waste land. He said, 'Hey, you!' but she was past and gone, up the slope to the weir and over the river, her head bobbing above the parapet of the bridge. He said, 'What's got into her?' staring after her until she disappeared; then he shrugged his shoulders and lit a cigarette. He smoked it down to the stub, ground it under his heel, and laboured on with his heavy bike.

If it hadn't been for the bike, he would have turned back the minute he heard the familiar noise from the bus; sloped off and lain low till the trouble was over. But he was too tired to shove it all the way back to Turner's Tower, and he couldn't just dump it at the side of the dirt road. A dumped bike was fair game on the site: there'd be no removable part left by morning. Not altogether safe by the bus, but safe enough for tonight, he thought a bit grimly: no one likely to come prowling round with them at it hammer and tongs, loud enough to waken the dead, or at least bring the neighbours out for the free entertainment. Standing and staring, whispering among themselves – he felt his ears burn as he trudged along, keeping eyes front, running the gauntlet. Lousy, prying lot, why didn't they stick to the telly? Catch *him* gawping at someone else's private punch-up! Was that what the kid had been doing? Well, serve her right if she had; she'd got more than she'd bargained for. Gala performance tonight – he'd never heard such a row! She'd started on the pots and pans. Dad must be off form; he'd let her get her second wind, by the sound of it ...

He whistled through his teeth as he heaved the bike through the gap in the fence and bumped it over the tussocky ground. Not much further now. Just a few yards, shove it under the tarpaulin, then clear off till they'd finished ...

Sammy said, 'Oh, it's you!' and he looked up then, for the first time, and saw the three of them, standing beside the bus.

They had been watching him come, along the road, through the fence. Not even Sammy recognized him at first; in the gloom he was just a man, or a big boy, stolidly wheeling his bike, apparently unperturbed by the terrible sounds from the bus. Must be stone deaf, Robin thought. Or perhaps unafraid! Hope seized him. *Help coming!* Someone older and stronger ...

Then Sammy said, 'Oh, it's you!' and the boy looked up. He stared at Sammy, then at Robin. His face changed, and he dropped the bike with a crash on the ground. There was an answering crash from the bus, as if something equally heavy had been hurled inside it. Then a loud moan from the woman.

Their heads twisted round. The moaning became jerky, rising and falling as if she were being shaken backwards and forwards.

Kate began to moan too, a steady, soft, keening sound. 'Oh stop it, stop it, make them stop it.'

Sammy said, '*He* can. It's his Dad!' He ran to the Wild One and clutched at him trustfully. 'Please. You do something.'

The boy looked down at him. Then over his head, at Robin. He shrugged his shoulders and turned away.

Robin said, 'Don't go. Please. I'm – I'm sorry I bashed you.'

The boy's light eyes narrowed. He said, 'I never scared little kids. You didn't ought to have said that.'

There was another bang from the bus. The door opened. The

man stood there, naked chest gleaming in the light that streamed out. They shrank back, all four of them, while he crashed down the steps and vanished into darkness. They heard him for perhaps half a minute, stumbling and swearing along the river bank. Then silence, sudden and total.

Kate whispered, 'Has he gone? Can we get Squib now?'

Robin said nothing. He was holding his breath and listening. The night seemed to be pressing against his face, smothering him like a blanket.

She said, 'Robin. *Robin.* You said we'd do that!'

The blanket seemed to be coming into his mouth now, pressure forcing it through his lips, down his throat. He gasped and looked at the Wild One. 'Will he come back?' he managed to say. 'Do you know?'

The pale blue eyes shone for a minute; then went empty and cold, as if a light had been switched off. He said, 'Find out for yourself! Grammar school yob!'

'Oh,' Robin said. '*Oh.*' Nothing more to be said. Waste of breath. He didn't feel angry – his fault, after all! – only empty. His legs were like hollow tubes, stiffly jointed. They carried him up the steps and into the bus.

The mess inside! He thought, *Indescribable!* Then, *No it isn't, it would just take too long!* Bent cooking pots, broken china, one bunk dragged away from the wall, hanging lopsided. The woman was half sitting, half lying across it, her head thrown back. For one heart-thumping second, Robin thought she was dead, her neck broken, but then she began to struggle up and he saw blood pour from her nose. She gasped and fell back again, pressing a cloth to her face. He thought she muttered, 'Get out,' but she was in no state to make him. His pulse slowed down and he looked round, almost calm suddenly. The laundry basket was under the table. He whispered, 'Squib!' and dragged it out. He tore open the strap that fastened the lid and saw him, scrooged up at one end, his pale, cottony head drooping forward. He whimpered and screwed up tighter as Robin touched him, but this was no time for coaxing: Robin bent and gathered him up in a ball. He felt horribly light – all bones, Robin thought, like a big, dead bird he'd once found on a beach.

Kate shouted outside, high and scared. '*Robin!*' He turned to the door with his burden and saw the man coming: his bearded, dirty face, glistening shoulders – nothing else in the darkness. Kate's voice from somewhere, '*Run*, Robin,' but he couldn't, no chance to, the man was so close he could smell him. A strong, sour smell, like leeks. He dropped Squib, thrust him to one side, and hurled himself at the man, arms going like windmills. His glasses came off: he heard the crack as the man trod on them and his surprised, whistling grunt as he reeled backwards. Robin hit him, in the chest, in the stomach; then stumbled and fell, clutching his knees. *Couple of minutes*, he thought, *time for Kate to get him away*. He heard the man shout, felt a fist thud down on his back, but closed his eyes and hung on.

16

THE little boy lying where he'd fallen, limp as a rag; that dreadful man, shouting and swaying in a sort of lumbering dance, Robin clinging to his knees . . .

Kate was beyond fear: it was as if she had passed through some barrier. She was to be afraid later, remembering this terrible scene, but now, at the time, she felt only a strange, stunned surprise that seemed to slow her mind and her movements like swimming under water. She bent over Squib but her stomach hurt; she couldn't lift him. Then someone pushed past her, hauled the child to his feet and shook him gently, as if shaking him awake. The Wild One. He said, 'Get out of it now, clear off. Look, Sammy's here.' And Sammy was there, standing beside them. Kate joined their hands together and said, '*Run*.' Her throat was dry; her voice creaked like a rusty hinge.

She turned and saw the man bending over Robin, dragging him loose, lifting him. He hung in the man's grasp like an old coat, and Kate's throat cleared. She shouted, 'Let him go, let him go this minute,' and would have run forward if the Wild One hadn't stopped her, pinning her elbows back.

He whispered in her ear, 'S'all right, he won't hurt him.' She twisted round to look in his face and saw he was grinning. He said, 'He's not *crazy*, my Dad . . .'

The man dropped Robin in a heap on the ground and looked towards them. He couldn't have seen them clearly as the light was pouring out of the bus and into his eyes but Kate held her breath and stood like stone. He stepped over Robin, climbed the steps of the bus, and looked in. Silence for a moment, stillness and silence, and then he said, 'God damn this rotten life.'

Kate thought these were the saddest words she had ever heard. Her mouth was dry and rough inside; when she breathed in, the air seemed to slice at her tongue like a knife. The man came down the steps and passed within two yards of her but she wasn't afraid of him, only sorry. So sorry, she felt as if something were bleeding inside her. He slumped off, shambling and heavy like a tired, old bear, and she watched him out of sight.

Robin was sitting up, feeling the ground about him. His shirt was torn and there was a red mark on one cheek. He said, 'My *glasses* . . .' Kate bent to look; he squinted up at her and said, crossly, 'I'll find them. You see to the kids.'

They had run off in the direction of the road. The man had gone the same way. He wouldn't hurt them, she was sure of that now, but they would be frightened. She ran after them, down the rough slope, through the paling fence. The moon had come up clear and steady in the sky, turning the pit machinery into marching, black monsters, and shining silver on the water. The man was nowhere to be seen. Nor were the children. She called softly, 'Sammy . . .'

No answer. They must be hiding. But where? There was no cover near, except the reeds at the edge of the pit. She walked slowly forward, along the narrow spit of land between the lake and the river. Then stood, listening. Water was chuckling somewhere, like a boat moving. She moved in the direction of the sound, through sharp reeds, tall enough to flick her face. Her feet squelched in soft, sinking mud. No firm ground anywhere . . .

She tried not to think of this, though it frightened her: the cold mud round her ankles, sucking her down. But if they were hiding in the reeds, they would be frightened too, hearing her coming towards them. She said loudly, 'It's only me, Kate. Where are you?'

Her voice seemed to raise echoes. *Kate.* Or was it someone else shouting? She stopped to listen again but then something moved in the reeds just behind her and plopped into the water

with a neat, finished sound like a cork coming out of a bottle. She thought, *A rat, I might have stepped on it*, and the horror of this shut out everything else: she stumbled blindly on through the swamp, tripped over something, lost her balance . . .

She fell almost on top of Sammy. He said reproachfully, 'Kate, you're squashing me!' He was sitting on a silted up clump of reeds in a little clearing at one end of an old pontoon. She put her hand on it to help herself up and it shifted sickeningly in the water. Sammy said, 'You'll joggle Squib, do be careful,' and she saw he was at the far end, huddled up in the flat bottom.

She sank down beside Sammy. He said, 'He's a naughty boy. I told him it was naughty to go in the boat but he wouldn't listen.'

She said, 'Didn't you hear me calling you? Why didn't you answer?'

'I thought it was Mum,' Sammy said. 'She'd be cross with me. I'm not allowed near the water.'

'How could it be Mummy? Mummy's not here.' She spoke absently, watching Squib. He was sitting quite still: he was safe enough as long as he sat still. But the pontoon was shallow and low in the water. If he stood up suddenly, got frightened . . . She looked at the black surface of the pit and shivered. She must be careful not to frighten him. She said gently, 'It's all right, darling. No one's going to hurt you.'

He didn't answer, didn't even look up, and this hurt *her*. She had found him, found him at last, and he wouldn't look at her! She said, to Sammy, 'You stay here, don't move,' and stepped carefully into the boat.

He did look at her then. Looked up. In the moonlight, his face was a blank piece of paper with holes cut for eyes.

She said, 'It's all right. You're all right. I've come to rescue you and take you home.' She stretched out one hand to him and the boat moved under her. He made a small, squeaky, frightened sound, and stood up. She said, '*Don't* . . .' but too late. He tottered, arms wildly waving, and then fell backwards, into the water.

She whimpered, 'No, no, please no . . .' but went after him at once, jumping from the side of the pontoon. Her feet jarred on the gravelly bottom and then the ground seemed to slip away and she sank deeply down. Drums beat in her ears. She came up, spluttering and spitting, her hair in her eyes. She flicked it back and saw him – only a few yards distant but dog-paddling steadily away from her, away from the bank. It was deep in the middle of the pit. There were supposed to be whirlpools. People had drowned there. She tried to call out, to warn him, but the words wouldn't come. Someone else was calling though. 'Kate, Kate . . .' As if they called out in a dream . . .

She looked back at the bank and thought she saw figures there; dark shapes waving, beckoning . . .

Not real, of course. People in a dream. She turned away from them and swam after Squib. She could see his small head, still poking up, but he seemed further away now. And she couldn't swim, or not properly; her stomach ached so much.

Cramp in her stomach. And fear in her mind – they said at the hospital that her scar had healed nicely, but suppose it hadn't? Suppose it opened up? The thought seemed to paralyse her; her legs wouldn't work. She drew a deep, sobbing breath, swallowing water, and threw her arms up.

There was something beside her. Something huge, like a submarine surfacing. She thought, *A whale in the lake, a monster.* She gasped and splashed in terror and Mrs Tite said, 'Don't panic now, put your hand on my shoulder.'

But she couldn't. Didn't want to. And not just because she was so tired. If he was going to drown, she wanted to drown too. She didn't want to be the one saved. Not this time . . .

She gasped, 'Get Rupert. Not me.'

Mrs Tite grunted something. Then her hand came up under Kate's chin, fingers pinching her nose, and forced her head backwards, under the water. Down, down – Kate fought to get free but not very hard: a kind of weakness, or weariness, seemed to be spreading through her. It wasn't an unpleasant feeling: warm water all round her and a soft singing in her ears and this gentle, drifting drowsiness as if she were on the edge of sleep . . .

When I wake up, I'll be dead, was her last, conscious thought.

To the watchers on the shore, it was all over very quickly. Neither child was far from the bank, and they were quite close together. A minute's struggle with Kate, but the little boy was sensible: he wound his hands in Mrs Tite's hair and rode on her back, high out of the water. No need for anyone else even to get their feet wet: Mrs Tite rose up in the shallows and stumped on to dry land, a vast dripping figure with a child under each arm.

17

'PRUE is the only one of you with any sense,' Mrs Pollack said.

That was the last thing Kate really heard or understood for some time: her mother's angry voice. Angry because she'd been frightened, of course, but what she said burned into Kate's mind. She must have said other things too but Kate couldn't remember them. She couldn't remember anything very much; only odd, disconnected things that might have happened in a dream. Being so cold, so wet; the smell of wet clothes, and someone crying. She thought, *Lost in a wood.* But she wasn't in a wood, she was in a car and he was there too, safe in the back. She put out her hand to him but it was Sammy she touched. He said, 'Kate, you're all wet, don't tickle me.' Then Sammy was gone, *he* was gone, and she was alone, in bed. The curtains were drawn and the light was on. There was a shade over the light. Her body was on fire and she couldn't breathe. Her mother said, 'My poor darling.' She was gentle and loving now. She gave Kate ice to suck, washed her with a cool cloth, tied back her hair. She stayed with Kate most of the time; when she had to go out of the room she gave her a bell to ring, a brass lady with a clapper under her skirt that felt nice and cold to touch. Mrs Tite had lent it to them; it had belonged to her father. Mrs Tite came to see her. And the doctor. His round, strawberry-coloured face seemed to wobble above her bed like a balloon on a string and he gave her injections in her bottom. His voice boomed like a foghorn. 'Just a prick, old lady.' The prick, and the stuff going in, and then she was floating away, soft and weightless as if her limbs were filled with cotton wool . . .

Dying must be like this, she thought. Feeling tired and light and pleased to be floating away. But she wasn't dying. She had just swallowed some dirty water from the pit and it had made her ill. 'Soon have you on your feet again,' was what the doctor said.

She woke one morning. It must be morning because her bedroom faced east and the sun was coming in: it lay across her feet like a sword. She watched it for perhaps a minute before she realized that she felt quite ordinary again, if a bit tired and empty. Her mind was empty. Then her mother's voice sounded in it. *Prue is the only one of you with any sense.*

What had Prue done that was so sensible? It wasn't fair to have said that. They had stayed to rescue Squib but Prue had been frightened and run away. She thought of her mother's picture: Prue running away from the pit. Her mother came in and she said, 'Did you finish the book?'

Her mother's face was pale and puckered up like a handkerchief that needed ironing. For a moment she looked as if she were going to cry, but then she smiled instead. 'Oh, you're *better*! Yes, it's almost finished. Just one more drawing.'

Kate said, 'I meant reading it. What was frightening, in the wood? Did you find out?'

Her mother looked puzzled. Perhaps it seemed odd that this should be the first thing Kate wanted to know! She said, 'Oh robbers, buried treasure, that sort of thing. Not much sense to it, really.'

Kate began to cry. 'You said Prue was the only one of us with any sense!'

'Oh, Kate . . .' Her mother sat on the edge of the bed and took her hand. 'I'm sorry, darling. I only meant Prue did the right thing, going for her mother. It wasn't the sort of situation children could deal with. What did you and Robin think you were up to?'

Kate felt herself blushing. She could remember what she had thought but not how she had felt. And what she had thought was just a story, like robbers and buried treasure. She said, 'Robin thought he'd been kidnapped. It sounds silly now.'

'It's the sort of thing a boy might think.'

Her mother looked at her. Her expression was shy, as if she wanted to say something else but didn't know how to begin. She sat there, one hand holding Kate's, the other tracing a pattern on the bedspread. At last she said, 'Rupert is dead, my darling.'

Kate felt embarrassed, nothing more. The sort of embarrassment you feel when grown-ups talk about the funny things you said or did when you were younger.

She wriggled her shoulders and said, a bit crossly, 'Oh, I know that. I knew it all the time, really.'

Her mother turned her hand over and looked thoughtfully at the palm. She said, 'I told you that picture was a bad likeness, I was never happy about it. Do you miss him very much?'

'I don't know.' Kate thought about it. Then she said, 'No. I just missed having someone. There was Hugo, but he was only a baby. Squib was the right age, and he didn't seem to belong to anyone.'

Her mother folded her hand up and held it tight between both of hers. Tight against her chest. She said, 'His real name is Henry Lincoln Gladstone McTavity. And you're right, he doesn't belong to anyone. His parents were killed in a plane crash about six months ago.'

Kate stared at her. 'But those awful *people* . . .'

'She was some relation. His mother's cousin, I think. There wasn't anyone else, so she took him over. She meant to be kind, perhaps.'

'*Kind?*'

'Well, not as it turned out. She wasn't used to children. She'd never had any of her own. She kept him clean and fed but she treated him like a puppy, shutting him up to stop him being a nuisance. She'd left her husband and got that job at the Tower, but when they sacked her she had to go back to him.'

'But what about *Squib*? Has *he* had to go back?'

Mrs Pollack shook her head. 'He's been taken into care.'

That *sounded* nice. Kate said, 'What does it mean?'

'Not an orphanage. A foster mother, probably. Someone who'll love him and comfort him. In fact . . .' She stopped; she had seen the question form in Kate's eyes. She said, 'No, Kate. I'm afraid not me.'

'I'd look after him.'

'You have to go to school.'

'So does he. I could take him in the morning and fetch him and bring him home and give him his tea and put him to bed. He wouldn't be any trouble, I promise. I'd wash his clothes and make his bed and keep him quiet while you were working. Oh, *please* . . .'

Her mother sighed. She looked as if she were thinking about it and Kate waited, so excited she could hardly breathe. Then Mrs Pollack said, slowly and gently, 'It's no good, darling. I'm just not the right sort of person.'

Kate lay on her back and closed her eyes.

Her mother said, 'I've got you. I don't want anyone else. That wouldn't be fair to him, would it?'

Kate didn't answer. Couldn't answer. If she tried to speak she would choke . . .

Her mother bent over her and stroked her hair. She said, 'Darling, I really am sorry. I can see it would be nice; like a story. But in real life there aren't any right true happy endings. You have to get used to things as they are.'

18

BUT there was a happy ending after all.

Robin came. Kate was out of bed and sitting by the window doing a jigsaw puzzle. She said, 'Hallo,' and went back to it.

Robin stood, watching her. Mrs Tite had said, 'Try and cheer her up, now. Her mother's half out of her mind with the worry.'

He found a bit of blue sky and fitted it in for her. It was a very babyish wooden puzzle of dressed up rabbits having a picnic. He thought, *She's too old for that, she must have fished it out of her toy cupboard.* He said, 'I've been to Court about Squib.'

Kate said nothing. She didn't even look up.

He said, 'I had to give evidence about her tying him up. Not what Sammy and Prue told me, that's hearsay and doesn't count. I had to tell just what I'd seen. All it was really about was the strap of the basket being fastened when I found him in the bus.'

He stopped. He had thought this would cheer her up. It had been so exciting – the most exciting thing that had ever happened to him. The magistrates sitting there on the Bench; two old gentlemen and a lady chairman in a hat. Swearing on the Bible and speaking up clearly and all those people listening . . .

But Kate still said nothing. She was concentrating on the bottom half of the puzzle, putting the green grass together. Perhaps, being so ill, she had lost interest in Squib. Or didn't feel up to talking about him, anyway . . .

He said, 'D'you know something? Emerald's moved into Sophie's house. She'd been looking for a place for a long time, they'd got a nice flat but she wanted a garden. So soon as Mum heard they were leaving next door, she went down to the agent and got the first offer.'

Kate said, 'That'll be nice for your Mother.' She spoke in her private-school voice: very polite, but distant.

'I suppose so. They've always been thick as thieves, those two. Not so much fun for me, though. More kids, running in and out all the time. Especially now . . .' He waited for her to ask him what he had meant, but she didn't seem to be listening. She had fitted in the last piece of grass and was staring at the wall. He thought, *Might as well talk to the wall!* He said, 'Of course, it'll look a bit different once they've got it fixed up. Colour on the walls and furniture downstairs – you know what it was like. Bare as a hutch, and all that white paint.'

'I liked it,' Kate said.

'Oh. Well. Each to his taste, as they say in French.'

She didn't even smile.

He sighed and said, 'Chacun à son gout. Emerald's got a new three piece suite. She said, now she's got somewhere to sit, perhaps you'd like to come to tea.'

'No thank you,' Kate said.

She didn't want to go anywhere. She wanted to stay where she was, in her own bedroom, doing all her old jigsaw puzzles, reading all her old books. They belonged to her. They wouldn't go away.

Robin remembered another thing his mother had said. He cleared his throat. 'Oh, do come on, Kate, don't be so *broody*. It'll take you out of yourself.'

'I want to stay inside myself, thank you very much,' Kate said. 'It's the most comfortable place to be.'

But she went, all the same. It would have been rude not to. If you couldn't be anything else, neither happy nor sad, you might as well be polite.

Sophie's house looked different. Tricycles and toys scattered over the neat front garden; the tiny hall so crammed with furniture that they could barely get in the front door.

'Some of this has got to go upstairs,' Robin said. 'Only the wardrobe's too big. Dad's got to take it to bits.'

They squeezed past the wardrobe that seemed meant for giants. Surely even Emerald didn't need a wardrobe that large? Perhaps big people just naturally liked big furniture, Kate thought, but where would they put it all, in this cottage? Not that she cared, really; she didn't seem to care about anything. She felt knotted inside; tied up tight, like a parcel.

The downstairs room was filled with an enormous, cushiony sofa with a flowered cover, and two matching chairs. Emerald's babies were building a brick tower on the patch of floor that remained and Emerald was sitting in one of the chairs, with Squib on her lap. His cheek was pressed against her and he was sucking his thumb.

Kate said, '*Oh!*' She stood, staring, and felt herself go red.

Robin was looking at her. He began to laugh.

Emerald said, 'Not too much noise now. That's why I told mother to keep Sammy and Prue away for a bit till he's settled. He's not quite sure where he is yet. Ate his dinner all right, but not a peep out of him. Not a smile, not a word.'

Kate knelt in front of him. He glanced at her, one quick look. Then buried his face.

Emerald said, 'He'll need a lot of attention, I can see that. Your mother says you're good with little ones, Kate. I'd be glad of a hand, now and then.'

Kate nodded. The knots inside her were loosening and she felt weak and floppy, but so happy ... She touched Squib's knee with one cautious finger. She said, 'Hallo there.'

He didn't answer. He pressed himself against Emerald's chest as if he were trying to burrow into her.

Emerald said, 'Come on, Henry.' She smiled at Kate. 'Henry Lincoln Gladstone. What a mouthful!'

Kate looked at the little boy, named after an American

President, and English Prime Minister. She thought, *Perhaps he's forgotten!*

She said, 'That's not his name anymore. Least, not the one he answers to. His name's Squib.'

'That's not a name,' Emerald said.

But the little boy had stirred on her lap. He squirmed a bit, and sat up. He still clutched the front of Emerald's dress with one hand, but he had turned his head and was looking at Kate. One blue eye, one brown, steadily staring.

She said, 'Hallo Squib,' and he began to smile.

CARRIE'S WAR★

The Second World War rages on, but Carrie, tucked away in a Welsh mining village, is more concerned with the rights and wrongs of the quarrel between her scrimping, miserable host, Councillor Evans, his mysterious sad sister, and the wonderful loving Hepzibah.

THE WITCH'S DAUGHTER

All the children were frightened of Perdita, until Tim and his blind sister Janey came from the mainland along with the sinister Mr Jones. A fine story about two lonely girls and it is also an exciting mystery.

THE PEPPERMINT PIG★

Johnnie was just a little runt, a peppermint pig, which cost Mother a shilling, but somehow his great naughtiness and cleverness kept Poll and Theo cheerful even though it was one of the most difficult years of their lives.

THE SECRET PASSAGE

Life was boring for the three children, living with their disagreeable aunt, after their happy home in Africa, but all is changed with the discovery of the secret passage.

REBEL ON A ROCK

Twelve-year-old Jo, on holiday with her family, stumbles into a revolutionary plot and decides to try and prevent its execution.

KEPT IN THE DARK

The three children's visit to their grandparents was every bit as odd and scary as they had feared: no one seemed to know who the mysterious David was and where he came from – except Grandpa and he wasn't telling.

*Now available in the U.S.A.